ALLISON

JEFF STRAND

For more information about the author, visit JeffStrand.com

Subscribe to Jeff Strand's free monthly newsletter (which includes a brand-new original short story in every issue) at http://eepurl.com/bpv5br

ISBN: 9798626465396

PROLOGUE

THIRTY-FIVE YEARS AGO

Dad set down his book and frowned. Nobody should be knocking on the cabin door at all, much less this close to bedtime. It was a loud knock, like somebody was in trouble.

They rented this cabin every year so that Mom and Dad could escape the stress of their jobs. They both worked where people were angry a lot, so they'd come out here for one week each summer, far from everybody else. "I get to be with the two people in the world I actually like," Dad would say, though he'd grin when he said it, because he liked plenty of other people.

Mom would paint and take lots of walks. Dad would bring a giant stack of books and rarely leave his recliner except for meals, bed, and the outhouse. Allison would read and draw and take walks with Mom and make up songs and play games and write stories and do whatever she wanted from moment to moment. She loved it out here.

Dad got up and walked over to the door. "Can I help you?" he called out.

"We're lost," a man said on the other side.

Dad sighed and opened the door. Somebody on the front porch pushed him so hard that he almost fell. He hadn't even regained his balance before two men walked into the cabin. One had greasy black hair and the other had greasy blond hair. Both of them had guns.

Allison screamed.

"Shut that kid up or you know what happens," said the man with black hair, pointing his gun at Mom. The man with blond hair already had his gun pointed at Dad.

Allison dropped her crayon and hurried over to Mom's chair. Mom put her arms tightly around her.

The men might have been brothers. Their faces looked the way Dad's did at the end of the week, since he didn't shave while he was on vacation. They were covered in sweat but shivering as if they were cold. Their clothes were dirty and torn and they could have been wandering out in the forest for a long time.

"We didn't want this," said the man with blond hair. "It's not our fault you never left. If you'd gone somewhere, just for a few minutes, we could've come in and nobody would have to get hurt."

"Nobody still has to get hurt," said Dad. "What do you want?"

"What do you think we want?" The man acted like it was the stupidest question he'd ever heard. "Money. And everything else valuable you've got in here."

The black-haired man walked over to Mom's chair, keeping

the gun pointed at her. "You've got a wedding ring, right? Give it here."

Mom immediately tugged on her ring. It wouldn't come off.

"Are you playing around with me?" the man asked, his face ugly with rage.

"Rings aren't supposed to just pop right off! I won't give you any problems." She pointed toward the kitchen area. "There's soap over there."

"We don't have time to screw around with soap! Just give me the ring before I shoot it off!"

Mom tugged on her ring so hard that it looked like she almost broke her finger. After the ring came off, she handed it to the man. He held it up to look at it more closely, then shoved it into his pocket.

"Your ring, too," the man with blond hair told Dad. Dad quickly took off his wedding ring and handed it over. "Now your wallet."

"It's in the bedroom."

"*Why's it in the bedroom?*"

"Listen to me, sir," said Dad. He was using the tone of voice that Allison recognized from when she got in big trouble, where she could tell he was trying really hard to stay calm. "I'm completely willing to cooperate with you gentlemen, but I need you to work with me. I get that you're desperate and I get that you're hurting. But my family and I were just sitting around in a cabin enjoying our vacation. Of course my wallet would be in the bedroom. It's not a trap."

The man with blond hair vigorously nodded. "Yeah, yeah, yeah, you're right, you're right." He pointed to the other man. "Go get it."

The other man hurried into the bedroom.

"It's next to the bed," Dad called out.

The man emerged quickly with the wallet. He tried to shake it open while holding the gun, but realized that wasn't going to work so he tucked the gun into the waistline of his jeans. He opened it up and took out a few bills. "What the hell is this?" he demanded, angrily shaking the cash at Dad. "There's like thirty bucks!"

"How much did you think was going to be in there?" Dad asked.

"More than thirty bucks!" The man stuffed the cash into his front pocket, then flung the wallet to the floor. He took out his gun again.

"We were never going to be a big score," said Dad. "You've got two rings and thirty dollars. Take them and go buy what you need."

"Or maybe we should kill all three of you. Tear this place apart. See what you're hiding."

"I just need you to be reasonable. How about our car? Take the car. It's parked about half a mile away. I'll give you the keys and tell you where it is."

The man with black hair pointed his gun at Mom and sneered. "How about we have some fun instead?" He licked his lips and looked at Allison. "How old are you?"

"Leave her alone," said Mom.

"How old?"

Allison looked him in the eye. "Ten."

The man chuckled. "Wow. I thought you were at least twelve. Big for your age. Ten, huh? That'd be interesting."

"The fuck's the matter with you?" the other man said.

"I was kidding!"

"You were kidding because I called you out on it."

"No, it was a joke."

"If I'd gone along with it, you wouldn't have hesitated. That is some diseased shit. You need to sort out your issues."

"It was a joke!" the black-haired man said. "I was trying to lighten the mood!"

"Why the hell would we need the mood lightened?"

"I—I don't know. Why not? It was a joke, okay? I'm not into that stuff. If you'd gone along with it, I would've shot you in the face."

"Are you threatening me?"

"No, I'm not threatening you! Be real! I'm saying that I made a joke and you took it seriously. If you don't have a sense of humor, that's not on me."

As the men argued, Allison noticed that Dad was glancing around the cabin. She thought he might be trying to find the closest weapon. She hoped he didn't do anything—the men weren't paying attention to him, but they both still had guns.

"Fine," said the black-haired man. "It wasn't funny. Let's just go, okay?"

"I'm not ready to go."

"You were the one calling me diseased!"

"Because you were going all pedophile and shit. The mother ain't ten years old." He leered at Mom. "What are you? Twenty-nine? Thirty?"

Mom didn't answer. She looked like she was about to cry.

"If you touch her," said Dad, "I'll kill you."

"Oh, you will not. You'll watch it happen and you won't do a damn thing, because even if you don't care if I blow *your* brains out, I know you don't want me to shoot your little girl. If you want, we'll lock her in the bedroom so this doesn't fuck her up too much."

Allison knew she had to use her power.

Her power frightened Mom and Dad. They didn't understand it, she couldn't really control it, and they mostly just tried to pretend that it was a figment of their imagination. But no matter how scared they were of what she could do, these men were much scarier, and she wasn't going to let them hurt her parents.

She couldn't just do it whenever she wanted. Only during what Mom called "intensely emotional moments." This was certainly one of them.

She looked at the man with black hair, *stared* at him as hard as she could, concentrated with all of her might, and tried to make him walk out the door.

He took a couple of steps backward, away from them. His eyes widened in surprise, and then he just looked confused, like he didn't understand what was happening to him.

He was still pointing his gun at Mom. Allison didn't like that.

The black-haired man very slowly lowered his gun. His arm twitched as he tried to stop this from happening. Allison wondered what it felt like. An invisible hand pushing down on his arm?

Then he shrieked in pain and dropped the gun as his arm broke.

It was broken *bad.* Allison could already see the blood through his shirtsleeve.

The blond-haired man, who'd seen everything, just gaped at

his friend. Allison's power scared Mom and Dad, and she'd never actually hurt them with it. These men had to be absolutely terrified.

Good.

She couldn't control her power enough to make them walk out of the cabin, so she had to destroy these men, make it so they couldn't hurt anybody else. It wasn't evil. She was protecting the people she loved.

She concentrated on the blond man's leg. It suddenly bent upward, breaking at the knee. He screamed and fell to the floor.

He still had his gun.

His other leg bent up and broke. That wasn't what she was trying to do. A broken rib shot up through his chest. That also wasn't what she was trying to do. She tried really hard to focus all of her attention on his hand with the gun. When all five of his fingers suddenly bent backwards until they snapped, she was happy.

His head twisted around and he stopped moving.

Oh, God.

Had she killed him?

Was she a murderer?

The black-haired man ran toward the door. Allison thought she should let him go—all she'd really wanted to do was get these men out of the cabin—but what if he came back? What if he hurt somebody else?

What if he told somebody what she could do, and Allison got locked up and studied? Experimented upon?

These were all good reasons not to let him flee the cabin. Though Allison also couldn't pretend that she wasn't simply *angry*.

She broke both of his legs at the same time. He fell forward and hit the floor of the cabin so hard that blood shot up from his chin.

She broke his legs even worse.

Then his arms.

She tried to split open his skull but couldn't quite make that happen. Though she did get him to smash his face against the floor a few more times.

Then, horrified, Allison realized that she'd lost control of herself. The blond-haired man was dead and the black-haired man was so badly broken that he couldn't hurt Mom, Dad, or anybody. She needed to calm down. She needed to stop.

She closed her eyes and took a few long, deep breaths. Her whole body was shaking, and maybe she'd have to go for a walk by herself to completely get this to pass, but the worst of it was over. She'd be forgiven. She'd had no other choice. Yes, it was nightmarish, but it was a *good* thing that she'd done. Maybe she was even a hero.

Allison opened her eyes. As she looked around the cabin, she saw the dead and broken bodies of Mom and Dad.

1

Allison Teal tried to figure out what to name her new cat. The poor little guy was skinny, arthritic, and had cataracts in both eyes. The people who'd either abandoned him or found him somewhere had just left him outside of the animal shelter, holding the end of his leash down with a large rock to make sure he didn't run away.

He hadn't tried to hide when Allison brought him home earlier that afternoon. He seemed to know that his opportunities for adoption weren't great and that he was getting a pretty sweet deal here. He'd gobbled down some dry cat food, done some exploring, and was now asleep and purring on the electric blanket she'd set on the couch.

The heartbreak of owning a pet that had already lived most of its life was coming—and Allison was devastated every single time—but it was worth her own pain to make this cat's last years happy ones.

At fifteen, she'd ended up with a foster family who didn't care if she got a dog as long as it didn't shit in the house. She'd gotten Smiley, an eleven-year-old beagle with one eye who walked with a limp. Her foster dad asked why the fuck she'd want *that* thing, and she'd said she wanted a dog that nobody else would love.

What she couldn't say was, "Well, Scott, I have these abilities I can't control and I'm scared that I might accidentally kill my own pet. If that happens, I want to at least be able to tell myself that I saved him from the gas chamber, and that he was still better off for having met me."

Allison was almost forty-six years old now, and she'd never accidentally killed a pet. She wasn't even sure her powers worked on animals. But she continued to adopt old pets (she disliked the term "rescue," which felt like she'd carried them out of a burning building), the uglier the better.

Only one at a time, though. Her house was no zoo.

The black and grey hair on his side kind of looked like a spiral. "Spiral" was a better name than "Ugly-Ass Old Cat." Maybe she'd go with that. There was plenty of time to decide; it wasn't as if she'd have any visitors to ask the cat's name.

She left Spiral on the couch and went into the kitchen to fix a snack. It wasn't a long walk. Her house was tiny, but she didn't need much space indoors. This house had suited her needs for the past ten years because it was isolated yet not *too* isolated.

She couldn't live too close to other people. Certainly couldn't live in an apartment. She couldn't take the risk of sobbing over the death of a beloved pet and discovering that she'd murdered her next-door neighbors. Intense emotions were what unleashed it. It had gotten her kicked out of one foster home for breaking another kid's arm—*only* his arm, thank God—and had caused various other problems in her life.

A couple of times she'd had to quickly pack up and move far away.

Allison had tried life as an all-out hermit for a while, and that simply didn't work for her. The company of a dog wouldn't keep her from going insane. A decade ago, with her financial situation relatively stable, she'd bought this small house on a large plot of land, with nobody else on her street, and kept mostly to herself. But when she wanted to make the short drive to Youngstown, Ohio, she could.

She'd never had a lover. Romantic relationships were incomprehensible for someone who had to maintain an even temper whenever she was around other people. She controlled her mood with prescription drugs, but unless she wanted to go full-on zombie, it wasn't enough.

No friends. Only casual acquaintances, just enough to have human company once in a while. If she got together with a group of friends and they laughed themselves silly at a hilarious anecdote, she could shatter somebody's ribcage.

She couldn't hold a regular job. This had been a real problem when she was first on her own, until she'd found work as a medical transcriptionist where she could do all of the work at home. She'd had to visit the office every day to drop off her diskette and pick up the new cassettes, but that wasn't a "high emotion" kind of thing. Now she had a full-time accounting job, one she could do entirely from home, with conference calls and webcam meetings replacing the need to go inside a building and interact with other people. It was high pressure, high stress work, but that was fine as long as the people who generated the stress were nowhere near her.

It was not a hell on earth existence, but it was certainly a disappointing one.

Her power was a total curse. No plus side at all. If she'd been able to move physical objects, she could've been a freaking superhero! She could've been the most productive, most famous construction worker ever. Or she could've been a magician, astonishing audiences with her "illusion" of moving things with her mind. Telekinetic powers in general would be awesome, but hers only worked on living things, and perhaps only on humans.

Maybe her abilities could provide some sort of benefit if she were able to control them. That would take practice...and how could she do that? "Okay, I'm going to try to refine my ability to raise your arm with my mind. I should mention that until I get good at this, I'll probably break your arm in a few places. Is that cool with you?"

Once, in the middle of a deep depression, she'd gone out into the forest and tried to practice on squirrels. It hadn't worked, although it was difficult to get close enough to a squirrel to be sure. Then she'd gone even further into her depression because of the self-loathing she felt from trying to experiment on living creatures. She wasn't simply cursed by her abilities; she was cursed by being an animal lover.

And even if she *did* become skilled at using her powers, could she ever truly trust herself to be vulnerable with somebody? What kind of genuine relationship could she have without high emotion? Not being able to argue with her because she could break a romantic partner with her mind...well, that would be a pretty big red flag for a potential mate.

That said, Allison could still go out in public. Have a nice restaurant meal by herself. Go on museum tours. Shop at the farmer's market. She wasn't hidden away in the shadows.

At home, she had books galore, the Internet, multiple streaming services, and plenty of nearby areas to hike. And she had Spiral. Some anti-social people might say she was living the dream.

So her life didn't suck. But it was certainly a letdown.

THE NEXT DAY, a staff meeting was scheduled for 10:00 AM, so it was one of the tragic days where she had to fix her hair and wear a bra. After going through the standard uninteresting agenda items, her boss, Jamison, let out a long sigh that didn't sound good.

"I'm sure the rumors are out there," he said. Allison, who didn't go into the office and thus didn't participate in office gossip, hadn't heard any rumors that would require a sigh before the discussion. She leaned forward, paying more attention than usual.

"I just want to assure you that the discussions of moving our work overseas are all very preliminary. No final decisions have been made, and we don't know that it would impact everyone, and I honestly haven't heard anything to make me think that they're moving in that direction in the near future. It's nothing that I personally would worry about."

Allison became a little queasy. She'd been through this before. When the boss felt compelled to address the rumors and didn't completely dismiss them, they generally turned out to be true.

"If I do hear anything, you'll all be the first to know," he said, obviously lying. "Again, don't lose any sleep over it, I'm sure everything will be fine, and there's no need to panic. Are there any questions?"

A couple of people had questions, to which Jamison gave insufficient answers.

The meeting ended, and Allison went back to work.

She had some savings, and she'd presumably get some sort of severance package, but she couldn't collect unemployment. Unless she was severely medicated—and going into an unemployment office on downers was not a recommended course of action—she couldn't put herself in that stressful situation. What if the employee was condescending?

She shouldn't worry about this now. It was way too early.

She didn't want to have to get a new job.

Stop worrying about it.

Allison needed a cat on her lap.

She left her office. She could work anywhere, of course, including outdoors, but she liked having a specific room that was only for her day job. Keep her professional life separate from her private life, so that she could watch a movie without feeling like she should be checking her work e-mail.

Spiral was asleep on the electric blanket. The heat probably felt good on his arthritic joints. Instead of risking total feline rejection, Allison picked up both the cat and the blanket and brought them into her office. She tried to sit down without disturbing Spiral too much. Her new cat stood up, stretched, then lay back down and returned to sleep.

Don't worry about your job. It's fine. Save your anxiety for when you know more.

She'd planned to go out for sushi after work (great happy hour specials; dine-in only), but she'd have to cancel that idea. She couldn't be around innocent people right now.

2

"It'll be fine," said Daxton Sink. "Just relax."

Sam tugged gently at his seatbelt. "I'm sick to my stomach."

"Like you're gonna throw up?"

Sam shook his head. "I don't think so."

"Give me notice before you do."

"I will."

"It'll be easier than you think," Daxton assured him. "You're just gonna shove a gun in his face and squeeze the trigger. Bam. Dead. We leave. Nice and simple."

"I guess so."

"You'll do fine."

"What if I freeze up?" Sam asked. "What if I can't do it?"

"I'll be there to make sure that doesn't happen. That's why he didn't send you alone. There's absolutely nothing wrong with being nervous. You *should* be nervous. You're about to take a human life. That's a big deal and it would be irresponsible of us to understate that. But I promise you it'll be fine."

"I guess it's just that I don't know how I'll react in that moment. You know what I mean? I have no idea how gross it's going to be."

Daxton chuckled. "Most of the mess happens on the other side of his head. Little hole going in, big hole coming out."

"I won't see any blood?"

"Well, you'll see some blood, I'm sure. But it doesn't get real gnarly unless your aim is off and you shoot somebody through the eye or the nose or something. You won't be shooting at a moving target. You'll press the barrel of the gun tight against his forehead, and then squeeze the trigger. Pretty much foolproof."

Sam nodded. "I just don't want to mess this up."

"I get it. You want to impress your future father-in-law. I'd feel the same way."

Sam's fiancé Olivia was the daughter of Dominick Winlaw. She was a scorching hot twenty-one year-old with an ass so spectacular that Daxton completely understood why Sam would forego pursuing his master's degree in elementary education in favor of doing dangerous jobs for Mr. Winlaw. Daxton certainly wouldn't mind being ten years younger and fifty percent more handsome; he'd try to marry that ass, too.

"You know, there's another option," he said.

"Yeah?"

"I'll kill him, and we'll say you did it. Tell Winlaw you performed like a champ."

"I don't really want to lie."

"That's fair. Just throwing out the offer."

Sam rode silently for a moment.

"Maybe in the actual moment we can see how I feel about it."

"Nope," said Daxton. "No way. We finalize the plan before we knock on his door. I'm happy to kill him for you, but it's not going to be a last-second decision."

"Yeah, okay, that makes sense. Sorry."

"We can work out the lie afterward if you want. If you feel good about it, we'll say that you shot him. If you don't, we'll say that he made a sudden move and I shot him. Winlaw won't be mad about that."

"I feel like I should do it myself, though."

"Your call. Just trying to be helpful."

"You know what? I really appreciate that. You kill him. I'll do the next one."

"Sounds good."

The GPS announced that their destination, an apartment complex, was one mile away.

"Killing people isn't fun," said Daxton. "Only a raging psychopath enjoys it. But I'm not gonna lie, if you handle this the right way, you can get a real adrenaline rush out of it. Not the part where you actually pull the trigger, but the stuff leading up to it."

"What do you mean?" asked Sam.

"We're there to kill him. That's the only possible way it ends. That poor son of a bitch has already been thrown off the skyscraper, and we're there to watch him hit the pavement. But *he* doesn't know that. So we mess with him a little. When we put the gun to his head, we tell him to give us the key to the safety deposit box."

"What safety deposit box?"

"There isn't one. That's the point. He'll say he doesn't know what we're talking about, and we'll pretend to get all pissed off and say that we'll kill him if he doesn't hand over the key. How will he try to get out of it? Will he keep insisting that there's no key and try to get us to believe him? Will he play along until he can figure a way out of this mess? We toy with him until it stops being fun, then we kill him."

"It doesn't sound like much fun."

"Maybe fun is the wrong word. Believe me, when you've got a scumbag shitting his pants in terror, it's a powerful feeling."

"*Is* he a scumbag?" Sam asked. "Nobody told me what he did. Mr. Winlaw said it was irrelevant. Do you know?"

Daxton shook his head. Truthfully, there was only about a fifty-fifty chance that the guy deserved what was coming to him. "No, but he was right about it being irrelevant. Not our decision to make. We certainly won't be murdering a saint, if that's what you're worried about. Maybe we should play it straight for this job."

He pulled into the parking lot of the apartment complex and drove to Building C. It was two in the afternoon and most of the spots were empty, so he was able to park right next to the outdoor staircase that would lead up to 207.

"Time to decide," he said. "Do you want to kill him, or do you want me to?"

"You can do it."

Daxton forced himself not to smile. He didn't get to kill many people. "I'll do the talking. You won't have to do anything but check the other rooms to make sure he's alone. If I *do* give you any other instructions, you obey them immediately, without question, like I'm a military commander. Got it?"

Sam really looked like he was going to throw up, and then perhaps burst into tears. But he nodded, unfastened his seat belt, and got out of the car. They walked up the stairs and went over to apartment 207. Daxton knocked on the door.

A thin, bearded man in his late fifties answered. Poor doomed Nate looked just like his picture.

"May I help you?" he asked.

"We'd like to come inside," Daxton said.

"We don't allow solicitors here."

"We work for Dominick Winlaw."

Nate's demeanor immediately transformed from "annoyed" to "sad and defeated." He nodded and stepped out of the way. Daxton and Sam walked into the apartment. Decent place. A lot of clutter and some boxes stacked against the wall, as if Nate was getting ready to move out.

Daxton immediately took out his pistol, which already had the silencer attached, and pointed it at Nate. "Have a seat," he said, gesturing to the couch.

Nate plopped down upon the sofa without protest.

"Are we alone here?" Daxton asked.

"Yes."

"If my associate checks the other rooms, he's not going to get a nasty surprise?"

"No."

"Check the other rooms," Daxton told Sam.

Sam just stood there, as if he hadn't realized Daxton had spoken to him. He looked ready to double over and vomit all over the floor.

Daxton snapped his fingers in front of his face. "Hey, check the other rooms."

Sam nodded and hurried off.

Daxton returned his attention to Nate. He had the look of a guy who'd known this was coming, and trying to move out of the apartment was only a half-hearted effort to escape the inevitable. They just looked at each other for a moment.

"Not gonna tell me I don't have to do this?" Daxton asked. "No offer to double whatever I'm getting paid?"

"Would it help?"

"Nah."

Sam returned to the living room. "It's clear."

"Good." Daxton aimed at the center of Nate's forehead, between the second and third wrinkles. Right before he was about to squeeze the trigger, he noticed that Sam had turned away. "Hey, kid!" Daxton wasn't old enough to think of a twenty-two year-old as a "kid," but he wasn't going to use his real name, even though the only witness would be dead in a few seconds.

Sam didn't look at him. "What?"

"You have to watch."

"Why?"

"Because if you're taking credit for the kill, you have to know what it looked like. If you can't even watch, then you need to tell your daddy-in-law that you're not cut out for this line of work."

"Okay, okay," said Sam. He took a few deep breaths, then turned back toward Nate.

Blood shot from the side of Sam's neck as a gunshot rang out.

Sam clutched the wound as a second shot got him in the back. He fell to the floor. Daxton caught only a glimpse of the woman as she ducked back into the hallway.

Shit!

Nate started to get up. Daxton shot him in the face, then hurried across the living room and pressed himself against the wall. He tried to ignore the gurgling, gasping sounds from Sam and focus only on fixing the more pressing problem. He slid across the wall toward the hallway entrance, ready to shoot at the first sign of movement. Nothing.

He peeked around the corner into the hallway. No sign of her. Two open doors and one closed one. He hadn't heard a door close.

How long until the neighbors called the police? This was supposed to be quick and quiet.

"I don't have to kill you," Daxton said, speaking at a normal volume. "I didn't see you if you didn't see me."

No response.

Daxton walked down the hallway. Door number one or door number two? If she was standing motionless just inside one of the rooms, gun raised, he'd have a problem, but otherwise, unless she was a fucking ninja, she'd make *some* sort of noise before she tried to kill him.

He waited, listening for any clue to where she was hiding.

Every second he stayed in this apartment made it more likely that he'd be caught, but he couldn't flee the scene with the woman still alive. When Winlaw had his meltdown, at least Daxton could say that he hadn't left a witness.

He stood silently.

Breathing. Quiet but rapid. She was in the room to the right.

Was she hiding or was she ready to shoot?

The kind of woman who would come out of her successful hiding spot to shoot at them in the living room was not the kind of woman who'd hide in a closet to await her doom. Daxton would hear if she was opening a window, so the only credible option was that she was planning to shoot him as soon as he stepped into the doorway.

If he fired at her blind, he might get lucky.

He might also get his hand shot off.

Worth the risk.

He quietly moved to the right side of the hallway. Switched the pistol to his left hand. And then, very quickly, he stuck his hand into the doorway and fired off three shots. As he pulled his hand back out of the way, he heard a body drop.

He carefully peeked into the room.

The woman looked like she was in her fifties. Nate wasn't married, so apparently he had an age-appropriate girlfriend. Daxton would've been happy just to have clipped her on the shoulder, giving him the opportunity to burst in there and finish her off, but two of the three shots had done some serious damage. She lay on the floor, eyes wide open in shock and horror, two expanding red splotches on her chest.

She hadn't dropped the gun, so Daxton shot her in the forehead.

He hurried back into the living room. Sam hadn't died yet, but even if Daxton called 911, it was far too late to save him. His neck was still spurting blood. He had maybe a minute left.

Daxton, hand trembling, took out his cell phone and called Winlaw.

"Is it done?" Winlaw asked.

"It went really, really bad," Daxton told him. "We need fixers here *immediately*. There's three dead bodies and a lot of blood. Two loud gunshots fired."

"Is—?"

"Yes, Sam is one of the bodies. I'm getting the hell out of here. I'll call you soon."

Daxton hung up the phone and fled the apartment.

3

Sometimes it was difficult to gauge Mr. Winlaw's emotional state. This was not one of those times. He was positively *enraged.*

"Do you know how much it cost to get fixers out there when the police could've been on their way?" he asked, pacing around his tiny office. Winlaw was extremely wealthy; this office was just for show when he played the role of Dominick Winlaw, small business owner. "You're lucky they went at all. You're lucky the cops didn't find the bodies. You should be in prison right now, and then I'd have to spend even more money making sure you got a shiv to the side. I can't believe this. I absolutely cannot believe this."

Daxton said nothing.

"I have to pretend that I don't know what happened to Sam," Winlaw continued. "Olivia will know that I had something to do with it, but I have to play this little game where I say that maybe he was a piece of shit who got cold feet and ran away. Do you understand what that's going to be like? Do you know the kind of strain you've put on our relationship?"

"I'm sorry," said Daxton. "I don't know how Sam missed an entire person when he was searching a two-bedroom apartment."

"Did he check the closets?"

"I don't know."

"Did you *ask* him if he checked the closets?"

"No."

"Then this is on you, right?"

"I assumed that he'd check every place a person could hide," said Daxton. "So if you're asking me if I mistakenly believed that he wasn't totally incompetent, then yes, it's on me."

"The entire point of you being there was to make sure there were no problems. Which means that I'm holding you personally responsible. This is one hundred percent your fault. Do you understand?"

Daxton decided that to continue to plead his case would serve no purpose. He simply nodded.

"You have a child on the way, right?"

"Yes."

"You'd better be the best goddamn father of all time, because that child is the *only* reason there's not a bullet in your skull right now."

Daxton completely believed him.

"How long have you worked for me, Daxton?"

"About six years."

"Wrong."

"Excuse me?"

"This is day one. Those six years of our relationship and the respect you had earned have been erased. We're starting from scratch. You're a new kid walking in off the street. And that applies to your pay rate, too."

Daxton almost started to protest, then caught himself.

"Also, before you leave this office, two men are going to beat the absolute living shit out of you, and you're going to just take it. They're going to beat you so badly that you should go to the hospital, though you won't. If you're not pissing blood, they haven't done their job. Am I clear?"

"How can I work for you if I'm hurt that badly?"

"It's not my problem. Consider it a couple weeks of unpaid leave. Then you will be on a severe probationary period where if you screw up in *any* way, I will Kirkwood you. Got it?"

Blake Kirkwood had slept with Winlaw's wife. Not when they were married—the sex had happened back in college, before Winlaw even knew his bride to be. But about three years ago, Kirkwood had tried to reconnect with Denise Winlaw when he was in town, asking her if she wanted to grab lunch and catch up. Kirkwood had spent the next thirty-nine hours and eighteen minutes in a soundproofed basement. The men who'd been down there—men who were happy to slice off somebody's thumb without losing a wink of sleep—refused to talk about exactly what happened, but it was "*bad, really bad—I mean, the kind of shit you can't get out of your head.*"

"I've got it," said Daxton.

Daxton was incapable of driving afterward, so the men (he knew them—Gary and Craig—though their previous friendly interactions apparently meant nothing when it was time to administer the beating) drove him back to his apartment. He hobbled up the four steps to the main entrance like a ninety year-old, then slowly made his way down the hallway toward his apartment, hoping Maggie wasn't home. He'd at least like to wash off the blood and change into fresh clothes before she saw him.

When he went inside, the television was on and he could smell coffee, so she was home. She stepped out of the kitchen, and her smile immediately vanished when she saw him.

"Oh my God, baby, what happened?" she asked, hurrying over to him.

She was wearing the maternity dress with the spaghetti sauce stain on the front that hadn't come out. Daxton had offered to buy her another one, but she didn't want to squander money on something she'd only wear for a few more weeks. When her stomach had first started expanding, she'd started wearing makeup more often and taking more time with her hair, but she'd quickly gotten over that. Now she didn't care how she looked.

"I'll tell you everything," said Daxton. "Just give me a minute."

"You need to go to the hospital."

"No. I'm not allowed to."

"You're not *allowed* to?"

"I said, I'll explain everything."

"What can I do for you?" Maggie asked. "Do you want me to start you a warm bath?"

"I'd love that."

She hurried into the bathroom. Daxton limped in there after her and began the excruciatingly painful process of removing his clothes. By the time he was done, the bath was ready, and he climbed in. The soapy water immediately turned pink.

Maggie picked up a sponge and began to gently run it over his shoulders. "What happened?" she asked.

"It was basically a babysitting job. Winlaw's son-in-law was doing his first hit, and I was there to make sure he didn't mess it up."

"Son-in-law? I didn't think Olivia was married yet."

"*Future* son-in-law, okay? It's not important to the story. He was freaking out and wasn't sure he could go through with it, so I told him I'd shoot the guy and give him credit for it. All he had to do was make sure nobody else was in the apartment. That's it. We weren't in some gigantic mansion—it was a tiny little two-bedroom place. Six-year-olds playing hide and seek could've handled that job."

"So somebody else was in the apartment?" Maggie asked.

"Why are you trying to get ahead of my story?"

"Sorry, babe. I thought it was obvious."

"Yes, somebody else was in the apartment. Lady with a gun. She got off two shots. Killed Sam."

"Oh, no. Sam was the son-in-law?"

"Of course Sam was the son-in-law. Who else would he be?"

"He could've been the person you were there to kill."

"How would that make any sense?" Daxton asked.

"She could've been your competition! I don't know how the story turns out!"

"You'd find out if you'd stop fucking interrupting me."

"Don't curse around our daughter."

"She can't—" Daxton decided that this was not the time to debate what his unborn daughter could and could not hear. "Yes,

Sam, my boss's future son-in-law, was murdered on my watch. I killed the target and the woman, and a fixer crew got everything cleaned up. So the job got done with no witnesses, but Winlaw blames me for the moron's negligence, and he had his goons do this to me. Told me we were back at square one. Gonna cut my pay. Threatened to torture me to death if anything else ever goes wrong."

Maggie ran the sponge over the back of his neck. "Jesus."

And then, out of nowhere, Daxton began to cry. Not just a couple of tears trickling down his cheek; he was sobbing like a little bitch. Maggie placed her hands on his shoulders and whispered to him like she was trying to soothe an infant.

He recovered quickly. "I think we need to run."

"What?"

"Not to Mexico or anything. California, maybe? Arizona? He wouldn't put *that* much effort into finding me."

"No. Absolutely not, Dax. My whole support system is here. You think with a baby on the way I'm going to run away from my parents, my sister, all of my friends? You think I want to change doctors? Are you out of your mind?"

"Were you listening to me? That whole part about me getting tortured to death? That little detail didn't sink in?"

"You said he threatened to torture you to death if anything else went wrong. So don't mess up again."

"I *didn't* mess up! You think I messed up?"

"You know what I meant."

"No, actually, I don't. What are you saying? Should I have held little Sammy's hand and walked him room to room, holding up the blanket while he checked under the bed?"

"We're not running away," said Maggie. "That's not an

option and I can't believe you even said it. What if your boss went after my family?"

"He wouldn't."

"You want to flee across the country because you think he'll torture you to death, and yet you're sure he won't harm my family?"

"Okay, yeah, I get your point," said Daxton. "I'm just not feeling good about things right now."

Maggie gave him a gentle kiss on the forehead. "If it was Sam's fault and he's dead now, there shouldn't be any more problems, right?"

"I guess."

"Winlaw said he'd kill you if something like this ever happened again. Well, Sam is the reason it happened. So you have nothing to worry about. Just do your job, do it well, and everything will be fine."

"Yeah," said Daxton. He sighed. "Yeah, you're right."

Maggie stood up. "I'll be back in a minute."

"Where are you going?"

"I need a cigarette."

"Seriously?"

"How am I supposed to quit smoking when you come home and stress me out like this?"

"Can't you at least vape?" Daxton asked.

"It's one cigarette because the father of my child came home and tried to take me away from my family. Sorry if I'm not feeling all Zen at the moment."

"Maybe just half of one."

"Maybe you stop bringing drama into our lives and I won't need any."

Maggie left the bathroom. Daxton couldn't believe he'd cried like that. How pathetic.

He wished he weren't so much in love with her. He could jump in his car and get the hell out of town. Never look back. Do whatever he wanted, whenever he wanted, and not have to worry about taking care of anybody.

But he was madly in love with her, even if she drove him to the brink of insanity on frequent occasions, and he wasn't going anywhere.

4

Allison decided to get the chocolate muffin.

She'd spent most of her life with the attitude that if she had to deprive herself of human relationships, she sure as hell wasn't going to deprive herself of delicious food. She got plenty of exercise; she could balance it out. Then, around the time she turned forty, her metabolism said "Adios, bitch!" and abandoned her. Walking around in the woods wasn't doing it anymore. She suddenly had to do horrible things like *not* order a chocolate muffin with her coffee.

But talk of the potential layoffs had continued for the past two weeks, with Jamison insisting that he knew nothing about it but that he'd let them know as soon as he had a whiff of news, he promised. Allison's intense stress had faded and now was just a mild but ever-present anxiety. There was no reason she couldn't pop a pill and leave the house for a while.

She got the muffin and it was everything she'd hoped it

would be. This little café made all of their pastries from scratch and you could tell.

Allison strolled down the sidewalk and did some people watching. An elderly couple walked hand-in-hand, all smiles. They didn't have the look of a couple who'd spent most of their lives together—Allison wondered if they'd found each other after losing their first spouses.

A teenager sat on a bench, watching a video on his phone, shaking with laughter. He was clearly self-conscious about it but couldn't stop himself. The video was simply too funny.

A young mother held the hand of her hyperactive son, who kept darting around and pointing to things that he excitedly wanted to tell her about. She was only half-listening to him. That was probably necessary to preserve her sanity.

A man walked out of his apartment building and held the door for a pregnant woman. He looked about thirty; she looked a few years younger. He had faint yellowish-green circles around both of his eyes, as if he'd had a pair of black eyes that were almost healed. There was a definite tension between them.

As the door closed, the man asked the woman something. She patted her pockets, then opened her purse and began to rifle through it. Allison, walking toward them, slowed her pace. They were random strangers but she was fully invested in how this all played out.

Up ahead, another man walked down the sidewalk toward them. Short. Thin. A little geeky. Mid-to-late twenties.

The pregnant woman kept digging through her purse while the man ran his hand through his hair, annoyed. He wasn't wearing a wedding band. He looked like he really wanted to say something to her but was holding back. Smart man.

A woman came out of the same building. The annoyed man and the pregnant woman stepped out of her way as she walked down the four steps and took a right turn, walking away from Allison at a quick pace. Not as if she was late for something—she just seemed like somebody who was used to walking fast.

Now the man did speak. Allison was close enough to hear it.

"Just forget it."

"No, I know it's in here."

"Just forget it, okay?"

"Fine. Whatever."

The pregnant woman closed her purse and slung it back over her shoulder.

She turned away from him.

Lost her balance.

She cried out in surprise, threw out her arms, and fell forward.

Allison, feeling an intense jolt of panic, lunged toward her.

Caught her by the shoulders.

Helped the woman regain her balance.

"Are you okay? Are you okay?" Allison asked, as the woman's boyfriend frantically asked the same.

The woman took a few moments to catch her breath. "Yes, I'm fine," she said. "Thank you so much. That was my fault."

"Thank God you were there," the man told Allison. "I can't even imagine how bad that could've been."

"You sure you're okay?" Allison asked the woman.

The woman nodded. "My heart's in my throat, but yeah."

Allison's panic hadn't subsided. It was growing worse.

Because though she'd caught the woman, about an inch had separated her hands from the woman's shoulders. The woman hadn't noticed, but Allison couldn't delude herself into thinking it hadn't happened. She'd used her curse.

She hadn't harmed the woman. But what about her baby...?

Allison stepped away from her as the tears started to flow.

"I'm fine, really," said the woman. "You caught me."

"Your baby—!"

The woman put her hands over her swollen belly. "I didn't hit my stomach. It's all okay. It was a clumsy moment and I'm mortified but nothing bad happened."

Allison shook her head, distraught. She felt like she was on the verge of completely losing it, which meant that she should probably get away from these people as soon as possible. The man was staring at her as if unsure whether or not they should praise her or try to escape the crazy lady.

"I need you to make sure the baby's okay," said Allison, fighting to get the words out through her sobs. "Go to the doctor. *Please.*"

"Nothing happened to the baby," the woman insisted.

"Make sure it's okay," Allison said. "Right now. Go get the baby checked out. Please just do that for me."

"Okay, okay. We'll go right in."

"Thank you. I'm sorry. I'm so sorry."

"You didn't do anything," the man assured her. "I mean, you're the *hero* here. Those were some amazing reflexes."

"Make sure your baby is okay. I may have—I might have—please let me know. Call me. I—I don't have anything to write with."

The woman took out her cell phone. "What's your number?"

Allison was so flustered and upset that she had to think

about it for a few seconds, but she recited the digits and the woman entered them into her phone.

"Call me as soon as you know," said Allison.

"I will. But it's all good, I promise."

Allison hurried off.

Maybe it was perfectly fine. Would a mother feel it if her baby's bones were broken inside of her? She would, right? She'd know *something* was wrong. Maybe Allison was panicking for nothing.

She didn't know what she could've done differently. She certainly couldn't have just let the pregnant woman fall down four stairs onto the cement. It was just bad luck, horrific luck, but it wasn't her fault.

Except that she'd left the house, she'd put herself in a position where something like this could happen, so it *was* her fault, and if she'd hurt that woman's baby she didn't know how she could live with herself.

Some people on the sidewalk were stepping far out of her way. She didn't blame them. She'd avoid the unhinged crying lady, too.

"Hey!" somebody called out behind her.

She ignored him and kept walking.

"Hey! Ma'am? You dropped something!"

She turned around. It was the short, thin, geeky guy. Allison waited as he hurried over to her.

"You didn't drop anything," he said. "I just wanted you to wait."

She spun away from him, but he grabbed her arm.

"I saw everything. You didn't hurt that kid."

Allison didn't answer. The guy took a wad of tissues out of his pocket and handed them to her.

"Thanks," she said, wiping her eyes.

"You should sit down."

"I'm okay."

"No, you should sit down. You've had a traumatic experience. C'mon, that bench is empty."

He walked her over to the bench. Allison almost considered pulling away and making a run for it, but decided that she really did need to calm down. They both sat down.

"I'm Cody," he said.

"Allison Teal."

"Pleased to meet you, Allison Teal." Cody shook her hand. "I'm not in the habit of talking trash about pregnant ladies, but she wasn't paying attention. It was one hundred percent her fault. It's like the guy said: you're the hero in this."

"All right." She wiped her eyes again, and then her nose.

"The baby's okay. You didn't even touch her stomach."

Allison shrugged and nodded.

"One hundred percent her fault," Cody repeated. "I saw everything. I saw it all."

Allison carefully looked at him. His tone was a little strange. "Excuse me?"

"I said I saw it all."

"I heard you. What did you mean by it?"

"I meant what you think I meant." Cody's eyes suddenly widened. "Oh, no, no, no, this is absolutely not going in a blackmail direction, I swear. I get that I sounded sinister. That's not what I was going for. I promise you that I'm a friend."

Allison stood up. "We're not friends."

"Please don't leave," said Cody. "I just want to talk to you. I shouldn't have said anything. I suck at talking to people. All I wanted to do is try to make you feel better. Don't go yet. Give me one minute."

Allison sat back down.

"You should go out to dinner with me," Cody said.

"Are you kidding me? I don't even know you."

"That's why I said dinner instead of marriage."

"No."

"I asked wrong. I didn't even ask—I just made kind of a statement. That was the wrong way to do it. Will you let me take you out to dinner?"

"No."

"Okay. I asked and you said no, so I'm not going to keep pushing it. We'll let that idea drop. In my own defense, a couple of minutes ago I saw a pregnant woman almost fall down some stairs, so I'm still a little shaken up."

"That's fair," said Allison.

"My minute's up, isn't it?"

"I don't know. I forgot to start a timer."

"I'm sorry if it seemed like I was trying to be menacing. I really wasn't."

"It's fine."

"Maybe I imagined it."

"Maybe you did."

"Anyway, you seemed upset and scared, and I just wanted to make sure you knew that you had no reason to feel bad. You should be feeling proud. That's basically all I have to say."

"Then I have two questions for you," said Allison.

"Sure. Let's hear them."

"First question: what do you think you saw?"

Cody hesitated. "From my vantage point—which I thought was a pretty good vantage point—it didn't look like you actually touched her. It was like...not levitation, that's not right. You know how when you've got two magnets, and they either stick together or they repel each other? It was like your hands and her shoulders were magnets, and there was this invisible layer between them. I didn't describe it very well but that's what I saw."

Allison kept her expression neutral. This was concerning, yet he did seem truly sincere about not having harmful intentions. He simply saw something weird and wanted to find out what was going on.

"Question two," she said. "Why do you want to take me out to dinner?"

Cody shrugged. "Spur of the moment thing. When I see somebody save a pregnant woman, I tend to think they might be a cool person to hang out with. Thought it might calm you down...although, obviously, first date jitters aren't all that calming, so I didn't think it through very well. Like I said, spur of the moment thing. I don't know. I wanted to ask you out."

"I'm old enough to be your mother."

"How old do you think I am?"

"Twenty-seven?"

"Twenty-nine. How old are you?"

"Forty-five."

"Okay, so, the math checks out biologically, but some people would be pretty unhappy about it. Not gonna lie—I thought you were a hot young forty-four year-old. Now it's awkward."

If Allison weren't still so upset about the baby, she would

have smiled. "Give me your number," she said. "I may or may not call you. If you haven't heard from me by five-thirty, then go ahead and make other plans."

Cody chuckled. "You're confusing me with somebody with a social life. My current plan involves an evening at home with a jigsaw puzzle. It isn't much different from my plans for the previous six or seven hundred evenings."

"Don't be mad if I don't call."

"I won't."

"I mean it."

"I won't be mad. I won't even ask you your favorite kind of food, because that would be presumptuous. We'll sort that out if you do call."

She entered Cody's number into her phone, shook his hand, told him that it was nice to meet him, and then got up off the bench. She walked away, feeling frantic, confused, and weirdly excited.

5

"Everything looks totally fine," said the nurse doing the sonogram. "You're not doing your daughter or yourself any favors by smoking, but you've got a healthy baby in there."

"So nothing has changed since our last visit?" Daxton asked.

"Not a thing."

"That's great to hear," said Maggie. "We didn't think anything was wrong, but I almost fell down some stairs, and we wanted to check it out just to be safe."

"Oh, of course. I'm glad you didn't hurt yourself. It can be tricky when you've got a new center of gravity."

As they drove out of the parking lot, Daxton put his hand on her leg. "Well, that's a relief."

"Yeah. I mean, I knew everything was okay, but the way that lady got so upset, we couldn't *not* check it out." She took out her cell phone. "I'll send her a text to let her know that she freaked out for nothing."

"Wait, hold up. Don't send anything yet."

"Why?"

"Hear me out," said Daxton. "What if we didn't let her off the hook?"

"What do you mean?"

"She thinks she might have hurt the baby, right? Irrationally, yeah, but she believes it. She kept apologizing. What if we did something with that? How much do you think we could get out of her if she believes you had a miscarriage because of her?"

Maggie let out a high-pitched squeak of a laugh. "How do you even think of something like that?"

"It makes sense, doesn't it? I show up with the bad news, give her a sob story about how we already didn't know how we were gonna pay our medical bills, and tell her that now you're insisting on having a funeral because you need the closure..."

Maggie laughed again and clapped her hands together. "That is *so* messed up."

"But the idea has potential, right? What if she's rich?"

"She didn't look rich."

"Let's say we get five hundred bucks out of her. That's still five hundred bucks we didn't have before. I'm not talking about a long con where we need a big score to make it worthwhile. I'm talking about one conversation that might end with her writing us a check. I bet I could be out of there in ten minutes."

"You'd permanently traumatize her for five hundred bucks?"

"I'd feel bad if it was for that little," Daxton said. He wouldn't really; hell, he'd do it for free, though Maggie didn't need to know that. "But it could be so much more. What if it's thousands? What if she empties her savings account to cope with her guilt?"

"You think she'll buy it?"

"Why wouldn't she? She's the one who flipped out and kept apologizing. You and I never said it was her fault or that the baby might've been hurt. That was all her. All we're doing is confirming her worst fear."

"I don't know," said Maggie. "I'm sure you could make it work, but the whole idea is just *so* freaking cruel. If she hadn't caught me when I fell, the baby could've been harmed for real. I'm not sure I can do that to her."

"You wouldn't be doing anything. It's all me. It's like when I do a job for Winlaw; you don't need to hear the details. I won't do a full recap. I'll just come home with the money."

"What if she finds out?"

"How would she find out?" Daxton asked. "She's not gonna go on some investigative journey. She's sure as hell not going to walk around our building anymore—I bet she avoids this whole neighborhood from now on."

"You can't promise that she won't find out."

"If she does find out, then she becomes a problem, and I'm really good at making problems go away. It's what I do."

"Yeah."

"So what do you say?"

Maggie frowned. "I don't know."

"It's easy money. We're not exactly shitting on golden toilets."

"Don't curse around our child."

"Sorry. We're not exactly pooping on golden toilets."

"What you're proposing is really awful. I can't let you do that to her for five hundred bucks. It's gotta be worth it. I mean, we're gonna destroy this poor woman. It's gotta be, like, two thousand or something."

"So if I can get two thousand out of her, you're okay with the plan?"

"Yeah, I guess," said Maggie.

"What if she doesn't have that much?"

"Then you tell her you made it up. Tell her it was a mean-spirited prank. I don't care what you tell her, but we're not going to ruin her life for five hundred bucks."

"All right, fair enough," said Daxton.

"When are you going to do it?"

"Tomorrow. We'll increase our odds if we give her a night to worry about it. Let her keep working herself into a frenzy."

Maggie giggled. "I'm not laughing because it's funny, I'm laughing because...I don't even know why I'm laughing. Yeah, let's do it."

ALLISON SAT at her dining room table, doing some online research on babies being injured in the womb. What she'd hoped to find was "Oh, yeah, the mother would totally know right away," but that didn't seem to be the case.

That said, as she sat here, an hour removed from her initial horror, she was feeling much better about the whole incident. She hadn't touched the woman's stomach. Not that she *had* to, but it wasn't as if every time she used her abilities people's bones started shattering. She hadn't been angry or frightened when it happened—just extremely startled. If she thought about it calmly and logically, based on her prior history, this incident had almost certainly done nothing to harm that woman's unborn child.

She couldn't completely relax until she got the call. But the idea that she was a baby-killing monster was no longer tearing through her brain, helped in part by the purring cat on her lap. Purring cats made everything better.

She had to figure out what to do about Cody.

She'd vowed that she would never again share her secret with anybody. But Cody didn't seem to doubt what he'd seen with his own eyes. He didn't know the full extent of what she could do, and he didn't know about the tragedies in her past, but he knew that she was either a very talented illusionist or that there was something strange about her.

Having somebody to talk to about it would be such a relief.

She could set the parameters. Explain that this could never be more than a "just friends" relationship (no benefits), and that he could never get her upset. The friendship wouldn't last, but maybe they'd be okay for a short while. She'd get dinner out of it, anyway.

She deserved that chocolate muffin, and she deserved to let this guy take her out to dinner. She'd wait for the pregnant woman to confirm that everything was fine, and then she'd call Cody.

THE WOMAN DIDN'T CALL.

It was 5:25 PM. Five minutes before Allison's self-imposed deadline to call Cody. Not that he'd refuse to speak with her after that, but she'd already come off as somebody who might not be in the best mental health and she didn't want him to think she was unreliable as well.

Allison kept wavering back and forth.

The baby is dead. They were so upset they couldn't call.

The baby is fine. They just haven't called yet.

The woman decided that a minor stumble was not a good enough reason to rush to her doctor, just because some crazy lady insisted upon it. As soon as Allison was out of sight, they'd decided not to bother.

Maybe the first option was true.

The second almost certainly wasn't. They wouldn't get her checked out and then be such assholes that they didn't bother to let Allison know that all was well.

Honestly, Allison was pretty sure they simply hadn't gone to the doctor. Maybe they couldn't get in to see their regular obstetrician and saw no need for an emergency room visit, or maybe they blew it off altogether. The pregnant woman would assume that she knew her own body better than the panicked lady who'd stopped her from falling, and maybe they had a busy day planned and simply weren't able to squeeze in a doctor's visit just for a stranger's peace of mind.

A text saying that they weren't able to make it to the doctor and would update her later would've been nice, but she didn't know these people. Maybe they were inconsiderate. Maybe they were worried that they'd wake up in the middle of the night and she'd be standing at the foot of the bed shrieking, "*Prove to me that your baby is okay! The spawn of our master must not be harmed!*"

Either way, though there might be an element of self-delusion involved, she'd decided that she was going to assume the baby was all right until she heard otherwise. They might never get in touch with her. She couldn't spend the rest of her life worrying about it.

At 5:29 PM, she called Cody.

"Hello?" he answered.

"It's Allison. From earlier today. The pregnant woman tripped, and you asked me out to dinner, and I said I'd call."

"I like how you think my social life is so rich that I need that many details to remember you."

"Well, I don't know you."

"Since my mom's picture didn't show up on the screen, it was either going to be you or somebody trying to sell me something. So thank you for not being a telemarketer."

"You're welcome."

"I feel like I'm not selling myself very well. I don't live with my mom or anything like that. I mean, not that there's anything wrong with living with your parents. There are a lot of reasons to go that route. I don't know who you live with."

"Just a cat. My parents died when I was ten."

"Oh, I'm sorry."

Allison cringed. *What the hell is the matter with you? Why are you bringing up your dead parents thirty seconds into your first phone call? You're anti-social but you didn't grow up in a goddamn cave! Jesus, learn to talk to people without being creepy and weird!*

"It's fine. I haven't been ten for a long time."

Yep, just keep on emphasizing how old you are, dipshit. How else can you get him to reconsider his invitation? Should you ask him what over-the-counter cream works best for an itchy crotch?

Cody chuckled. "So you said you may or may not call, which kind of implied that you'd call if you were interested, and wouldn't call if you weren't. I'm hoping that's accurate."

"It is."

"Hey, great! Did you hear back from the lady?"

"No. I'm just going to assume that everything's fine."

"That's probably the right attitude. Do you have a favorite restaurant?"

"What if we just got take-out and had dinner at your place?" Allison knew she might be sending the wrong message, but if she was going to tell him about her telekinetic powers, she didn't want other people at the restaurant to overhear. She wasn't worried that Cody might be a serial killer. If the evening went horribly, fatally wrong, *she* wouldn't be the corpse on the floor.

Cody hesitated for a moment. "Sure, that sounds fine. I'm a neat freak, so there's nothing to clean up. If anything, I should mess it up a little."

"What time works for you?"

"Anytime. Seven?"

"Perfect."

"What genre of food do you prefer? I'll have it delivered."

"Do you like Thai?" Allison asked.

"Absolutely."

"Order whatever you want. I like it all."

"Will do." Cody gave her his address, and Allison hung up.

Holy shit. She had a date.

She wasn't sure if she should have clarified the reason for wanting to do this at his place. "Just to be clear, you're not getting laid tonight," seemed inappropriate. If he started to get a bit date rapey, she'd set him straight.

But...she had a date tonight!

Holy shit!

6

Allison owned "don't care what anybody else thinks" clothes, and she owned "professional business attire for video conference calls" clothes. She didn't own "first date" clothes.

She very briefly considered going out and buying something, but she didn't even know where to begin. She needed a wacky best friend who could make faces while she stepped out of the dressing room in various outfits as part of a movie montage, finally giving her a thumbs-up at the end of the song.

She'd have to decide whether to go with the high end of her don't-care clothes or the low end of her business clothes. After way more contemplation on the issue than she would ever admit to anybody, she went with the former. Jeans and a nice red T-shirt. If he greeted her at the door in a tuxedo, well, at least her shirt didn't have grease stains on the front.

She looked in the mirror. Her clothes were fine, for

somebody who wasn't trying to impress anybody. Her hair...not great. It didn't look like vermin nested in it, but the proper description was "ugh."

There wasn't enough time for a trip to the salon. She'd just have to do the best she could.

As she messed with her hair, she felt like she should be far more worried about Cody knowing her secret than she was. She did have a bug out bag in the closet if she needed to flee, but she really hadn't thought about what she'd do if he said, "*I'm telling the world about your dark magic, wretched witch!*" That simply wasn't the vibe she got from him. Granted, one could argue that a woman who purposely didn't interact with other people might not be the best judge of these things, but she'd trust her gut until she had reason to do otherwise.

Her hair was clean and combed and she decided that was the best she could do. At least there were no twigs in it.

She gave Spiral a couple of treats to make up for having to turn off the electric blanket (she didn't want to burn the house down) and then left.

His apartment building was several miles from where they'd met. It was only 6:51, so she waited in the car for a few minutes, wondering if this was a terrible idea, and then headed up to his third floor apartment right on time.

She knocked on the door, still questioning this decision.

Cody answered. He'd changed his shirt, but he wasn't any better dressed than her except that he was wearing long sleeves. "Great to see you again!" he said, stepping out of her way without offering a hug.

She walked into his apartment. He wasn't kidding about

being a neat freak. The place was almost antiseptic, though it smelled nice, like a kind of flower she couldn't identify.

There was a couch, a very large television, and a couple of bookshelves. Without going over and perusing the contents, she was certain that they were arranged in a very specific manner. Alphabetically by author? By subject matter? She didn't know, but she was confident that there was a system.

There were also four small tables, upon each of which was a partially completed jigsaw puzzle.

"Wow," she said, walking over to the closest one, as Cody closed the door. It depicted what appeared to be a house on a lake. "You weren't kidding about spending the evening with a puzzle."

"Yeah," said Cody. "I usually have three or four going at once. Sometimes I want to finish one up in a night, so I go with a medium difficulty one. Sometimes I'll work on puzzles that take a few days, maybe a week to finish." He walked over to the furthest table. "I've been working on this one for months."

Allison joined him by the table. All of the pieces were just dark red, with no variance that she could see.

"That would drive me insane," said Allison.

"It's definitely a challenge."

"Is it fun?"

"It's satisfying. Pretty much any time you add a new piece it's a cause for celebration."

"Very cool."

"But don't worry, I wasn't going to ask you to do jigsaw puzzles. The food is on its way. Did you want a drink? I don't really do alcohol, but I've got water and about ten different kinds of soda. You may just want to look in the fridge."

They went into the kitchen and he opened the refrigerator door. He did indeed have about ten different varieties of soft drinks. She selected a regular can of Coke and he took the same.

They popped open their cans, took a drink, and stood silently for a moment.

"I'm really sorry about making it seem like I was trying to blackmail you," Cody said. "I can't stop thinking about that."

"It's long forgotten."

"Not by me. Did you want to sit down?"

"Sure."

They walked over to the couch. Allison sat down on the left cushion, and Cody sat on the right, leaving a full cushion between them.

"I guess I should tell you why I wanted to have dinner at your place," said Allison. "I could try to convince you not to believe your eyes, but I'm not going to do that. I wanted to answer your questions without anybody overhearing."

"I appreciate that," said Cody. "Full disclosures from both of us."

"You have a disclosure?"

"Not paranormal abilities, but yeah."

"Let's hear it."

"You first."

Allison shook her head. "You first, because now that you've said you have a deep dark secret I'm going to believe that you're an axe-murderer until you tell me otherwise."

"Maybe we should wait until after dinner."

"Maybe we should talk now so we can enjoy meaningless chatter over dinner."

"Do you know what night terrors are?" Cody asked.

"Really, really intense bad dreams?"

"Yeah. Just *horrible* nightmares, and you scream and you flail around and it scares the absolute living crap out of the person you're sleeping with, even if you warned them that this could happen. I'll have night terrors that are so intense that I'll wake up and not realize I'm awake. So if I'm dreaming about being strangled by spiked tentacles—a recurring dream, by the way—I'll wake up and still believe that I'm being strangled. It's like I can literally see the nightmare still happening. And sometimes I fight back against the monsters."

"Oh my God."

"Yeah. It's pretty hard to have a girlfriend when you have to explain that you might try to kill her in your sleep."

"I can see where that would be a problem."

"Yep."

"Sorry," said Allison. "I wasn't trying to be a smartass."

"Oh, no, that's a good reaction. I much prefer you being a smartass to you running for the door."

"So...*have* you tried to kill somebody in your sleep?"

Cody hesitated. "Yes."

"You didn't succeed, did you?"

"No."

"Did you hurt somebody?"

"Yes. I bashed her face into the headboard and wrenched her arm out of its socket."

"Oh." Allison had no idea how to react to this.

"Her nose was bloody but not broken, and the emergency room doctor popped her shoulder back in. I figured out where I was before I did worse. Obviously we're not together anymore."

"Was she understanding about it? I mean, you just said that you broke up, but did she understand what happened?"

Cody took a very long drink of his Coke. "I can't believe we're having this conversation so soon. We were supposed to be talking about *your* weirdness. I was going to save this for the third date."

"Too late now."

"No, she was not understanding about it. And that, Allison, is the exciting tale of how I spent thirty days in a minimum security prison."

Instead of being horrified, that revelation actually made Allison feel better about their date. She didn't want to bring instability and strange boundaries into somebody's life. "*We can't sleep together because I might think you're a spiked tentacle*" was a nice match for her own issues.

"I have to admit, that's not the kind of story I thought you were going to share," she said.

"By the way, this was a few years ago," said Cody. "I probably should have started with that. I'm not fresh out of incarceration. I've readjusted to society."

"That's good to know."

"So anyway, I tend to be a solo sleeper these days."

"Very understandable."

Cody smiled. "I wish the food had arrived and interrupted that story."

"It's out of the way now. And I haven't run for the door. Though if I see you start to nod off, I'm outta here."

"Your turn."

"What do you want to know?"

"The whole thing. I guess we'll start with—"

The doorbell rang.

"You're saved," said Cody, standing up. "That's so not fair."

He answered the door and collected two very large plastic bags. After thanking and tipping the delivery guy, Cody went into the kitchen and started removing various containers. Allison walked in after him.

"That's way too much food," she said.

"I wanted a nice variety."

"It's enough for eight people."

"Some of it's going in my refrigerator and some of it's going home with you. Nobody is going to make you gorge yourself. And if you do gorge yourself, this is a judgment free zone. But not really because it'll make me like you even more."

The plates and utensils were already set out on the kitchen counter. Cody opened all of the boxes and then they went down the line of containers, filling their plates with food that looked absolutely delicious. They sat at the dining room table.

"An actual table," said Allison. "This is a nice change for me. I usually just eat in front of the TV."

"We can eat on the couch if you want."

"I don't get the impression that you're a 'food near the couch' sort of guy."

"Oh, I'm fine with food near the couch. If you spilled something, I'd immediately attack it with cleaning supplies, but I wouldn't have a nervous breakdown or anything."

"Nah, the table is nice."

"Dig in."

Allison dug in. It was damn good Thai. She offered lavish

praise, and Cody said that this place had never let him down. When he reached for the bottle of soy sauce, his shirtsleeve rose a bit, revealing a scar across his wrist. Allison pretended she didn't see it.

For a few moments all they did was eat and discuss the awesomeness of the food. Finally, Cody said, "Okay, *now* it's your turn."

"You don't want to wait until after dinner?"

"I feel like your confession is more fun than mine."

"It's not," Allison told him.

"Your call. You're my guest."

"We can talk about it now. But I'm going to start with a question for you."

"Sure."

"You think you saw me exhibit supernatural abilities. That's what we're here to talk about. I confirmed them. Why the hell are you so calm?"

"Should I be screaming and pointing?"

"Something like that."

Cody shrugged. "When I wake up from a nightmare, I don't know where I am or what's really happening. It's terrifying. When I'm awake and outside the house, I am the most observant nerd you'll ever meet. I mean, your eyes and brain can always play tricks on you, but in that moment I was hyper-alert. I know exactly what I saw. When I confronted you about it, if you'd told me I was out of my damn mind and to go see a shrink, you might have gotten me to question myself. But you didn't."

"So I should have been ruder."

"Pretty much, yeah. I'm an open-minded skeptic. There *could* be aliens, and there *could* be Bigfoot, and there *could* be a God, but I haven't seen any first-hand evidence. There was a very clear gap between your hands and her shoulders. I saw it. You didn't convince me that I was wrong. So I'm very interested in hearing your story. If it seems like I'm being too calm, that's because I had all day to freak the hell out and get it out of my system before you got here." He took a bite of cashew chicken.

"That explanation works for me," said Allison. "And can I trust you to keep a secret?"

"If you're asking if I'm going go around telling people that I met a chick with telekinetic powers, yeah, I think I can keep that under my hat."

Allison decided that, yes, this could be a disastrous mistake, but she was going to tell him anyway. "I've been able to do this since I was a kid."

"You can move objects with your mind?"

"No. I can move people. But I can't control it."

"Move people how?"

"I can make people move against their will. So I could make you raise your arm, or I could mentally drag you into the kitchen."

"That's really cool."

Allison shook her head. "It's not."

"So you could move my arm? Can we try it?"

"Absolutely not. It's like I'm moving something very fragile, as if your arm was made of glass. I'd probably break it."

"Let's not try it then."

"If I practiced I could probably get good at it. But that would be like a newbie surgeon asking for volunteers so he can practice heart transplants."

"I emphatically do not volunteer."

"This is really good," said Allison, taking another bite. "I'm going to start ordering from here all the time."

"Never had a bad meal from them. So I guess the obvious question is that there's a *reason* you know about the 'arm made of glass' thing, right?"

"Was that a question?"

"It was phrased kind of like a question, yeah."

"Yes. I know what my ability can do. That wasn't guesswork on my part."

"You know what, I'm satisfied with that answer," said Cody. "We don't need to get into the bone-breaking details."

"Here's the full situation. If I try to use them, I can't really control them, so I don't try to use them. Under normal circumstances, like sitting here eating amazing Thai food, everything is totally fine. In moments of high emotion, if I'm really upset or I'm scared or I'm deliriously happy, they become involuntary."

"Oh, shit."

"Yeah."

"It's the 'happy' part that I'm going to zero in on. Like, how does that work? You can't enjoy your dinner too much?"

"I can enjoy food," said Allison. "But you couldn't make me laugh too hard."

"I'm glad I found this out before I started being too witty."

"I would've warned you."

"That...really, really, really sucks. You can't laugh too hard? That's just awful. So it's like living your whole life with a broken rib, except that you'd give other people the broken ribs."

"Exactly."

"I can't even imagine that," said Cody. "I mean, I spend most of my time alone, so laughing hysterically would be a sign of insanity, but still."

"Shall we take this one step further into Too Much Information?"

"Sure, why not?"

Oh, God, why am I telling him this?

"I can't have sex," said Allison. "I could never trust myself to have an orgasm with somebody else there."

Cody was silent for a moment.

"I can fail to make you come," he said. "That's not a problem at all."

Allison laughed, and then slapped her hand over her mouth. Cody looked horrified. They just stared at each other, until Cody finally patted his chest, arms, and legs.

"It's okay," he reported. "No broken bones."

"It would take more than that, but, yeah, that's my life. Aren't you glad you asked me out?"

"One could argue that it's a case of two messed up people finding each other."

"I'm still old enough to be your mother."

"I attack people in my sleep, you break bones with your mind—I think the age difference is one of the less weird parts of our relationship. How did you get these powers?"

"Not a clue," said Allison. "Just born lucky, I guess.

"Anyway, have we got all the heavy stuff out of the way?"

Cody hadn't told her about the scar on his wrist, and Allison hadn't told him about her parents or the others, but she felt like they'd confessed enough for now. "Yeah."

"What superficial stuff can we talk about while we finish eating?"

"Our jobs?"

"Ugh. Yeah, all right. I should warn you that I'll be talking about working in corporate information technology, so if you feel yourself getting over-stimulated, let me know."

They had a lovely conversation about much more trivial stuff. Allison ate way too much and didn't care. Nothing could ever happen between her and Cody, of course, but she was having a perfectly pleasant evening.

"I can't stay very late," she said. "I've got to get up for work in the morning."

"Yeah, me too."

"Wanna do a puzzle?"

Cody looked genuinely shocked. "Seriously?"

"Yeah. Not that red one from hell, but a normal person's puzzle would be fun. We don't have to finish it tonight."

"I'd love that. Obviously."

Allison had planned to leave by 9:00. By 9:45, they'd put together the frame and a significant portion of the pug's face. She felt like they could finish this thing up if they put in another hour or so, but no, it was time for her to head home.

"Thanks for hanging out with me tonight," Cody said, as he scooped leftovers from dinner into plastic containers. "If you decide that I make you dangerously giddy and think it's unsafe to see me again, you don't have to return the containers."

"I wouldn't mind coming back to finish this puzzle," said Allison.

"Really?"

"I need to see what it looks like when it's done."

"The—"

"I know the picture is on the back of the box. It was an

excuse to see you again. You said I didn't have to return the containers, so you ruined that excuse."

"Any time you want to come back, the puzzle will be here."

Cody gave her a hug at the door, and Allison went home.

No way could this work, but for now, it was fun to pretend.

7

Daxton didn't take a shower the next morning, and he put on the same clothes Allison had seen him wearing before. He didn't want to actually stay up all night—he wasn't a method actor and he needed his mind to be sharp—but he wanted Allison to *think* he'd been up all night.

He didn't shave or comb his hair. Clearly, he was too distraught over the tragedy to worry about his personal appearance. He did apply deodorant and brush his teeth, since he didn't want body odor or bad breath to distract her from her sympathy and guilt.

Before turning onto her street, he rubbed his eyes really hard.

Finding her house had taken a couple of extra steps—her address wasn't connected to her phone number—but it wasn't that difficult. It was a small house but she had a huge yard and no close neighbors, which was a pretty great deal. Daxton would love to live in a place like this.

He pulled into her driveway and tried to think depressing thoughts.

She had no idea he was coming. She might not even be home, although there was a silver Prius V in the driveway. After parking behind it, he got out of his own car, staying in character in case she happened to peek out the window. Head lowered, he walked up to her front door and rang the doorbell.

A few moments later, the door opened. It was her, in sweatpants and a baggy T-shirt. He assumed that the delay in answering had been for her to put on a bra. She looked extremely surprised to see him there, which was the whole point.

"Hi," he said, softly. "I'm so sorry I didn't call first. It just didn't feel like the kind of thing you say over the phone. May I come in?"

"Oh, yes, yes, of course," said Allison, stepping inside. He followed her, moving slowly but not trying to oversell it. "Can I get you something? Coffee? Water?"

"No, I won't be long."

Allison looked physically ill, as if she knew devastating news was on the way. Perfect.

"Do you want to sit down?" she asked.

"No, that's...actually, yes, I should probably sit down."

They went over and sat on her couch. Allison stared at him intently. Daxton said nothing. He breathed rapidly and looked at his shoes as if trying to work up the courage to speak, or as if he were having difficulty trying to find the right words.

"I'm sorry," he finally said.

"No, no, take your time. I don't think I even told you my name. I'm Allison."

"I'm Daxton."

"Hi."

"Let me just say right up front that nobody is blaming you, okay? Don't take any of this the wrong way. The emergency room doctors said you weren't being reckless. Anybody with a good heart would've done what you did. It's just that..."

Daxton put his hand over his mouth. He closed his eyes, as if unable to go on.

When he opened them again, Allison had a couple of really good tears trickling down her face.

"Is the baby going to be all right?" she asked.

Daxton didn't answer.

They sat in silence.

Daxton composed himself. "The way they explained it, if you hadn't been there, it could've been a whole lot worse, but she also might have caught herself or landed on her knees. It was the *jolt*, basically. Too much of an impact on the top half of her body instead of her legs. I still don't completely understand it. I felt like you saved her. But that's not what the doctors said. They gave me a written report but, I don't know, it's just hard for me to focus on anything right now."

Allison's entire body was quivering. It was difficult for Daxton not to crack a smile.

"So she had a miscarriage. I mean, I don't know what to tell you, I wish I had better news. It's just what happened. Thank God we listened to you when you thought something was wrong, because otherwise we wouldn't have been at the hospital when it happened. That's one good thing. I mean, my girl isn't doing well, not at all, but at least she's getting the care she needs. The financial stress of this whole pregnancy was keeping us up at night, but we could never imagine something like this happening." Though Daxton wished he could summon tears, he thought he was doing a pretty good job of sounding full of heartache and despair. "I honestly don't know what we're going to do."

Allison looked so horrified, so upset, that Daxton actually felt a bit guilty.

"I need you to leave," she said, voice trembling.

"I didn't come here to point fingers," said Daxton. "You asked me to tell you what happened, and so I'm here. You'll never know how much I wish I could come here and say that you saved our unborn child."

"I need you to leave *now*," said Allison. "You have to go. Please."

Daxton stood up. This wasn't the reaction he'd expected. He wasn't going to push her too hard, but he wanted to avoid a return visit if he could possibly help it.

"I understand," he said. "It doesn't even feel like real life. I keep waiting to wake up from this nightmare, but it's just not going to happen."

"I really need you to leave, I need you to leave now, I need you to leave my home now," said Allison, her voice going from frantic to hysterical. "You can't be here, you have to leave, please, you have to leave *right now!*"

An invisible force slammed into Daxton.

He hurtled across the living room for ten feet until he crashed into the wall.

He fell to the floor, gasping for breath.

What the fuck was that?

His ears were ringing so loudly that he could barely hear Allison shouting that she was sorry. He got to his feet and staggered toward the door, terrified. It took him a couple of tries to grab the doorknob, but he got it open and hurried outside. He ran to his car, started the engine, and drove off.

ALLISON COULDN'T GET up off the couch.

She'd killed the baby!

She was sobbing and having trouble breathing and it felt like her head might literally explode. She hoped that did happen. Let her head explode in a burst of blood and bone, preventing her from killing more babies in the future.

Oh God, oh God, oh God...

Spiral jumped up onto the couch. Allison gently shoved him away. She didn't deserve to be comforted right now.

She'd murdered their baby.

She'd gone out in public, knowing how dangerous it was for her to be around other people, and she'd acted without thinking, and she'd murdered their unborn child.

Those poor people were going to have a permanent hole in their lives, a tragedy from which they would never completely recover, and it was her goddamn selfish fault.

She had no idea what Daxton was planning to do. Maybe come back with an angry torch-wielding mob. Burn down her house while she sat here, unable to get up off the couch.

She just sat there, crying and trying to keep Spiral from snuggling her.

Finally she leaned forward and vomited all over her lap. And though she was in a bad, dark place right now, she wasn't going to sit here with puke all over her sweatpants. She stood up, immediately got dizzy, and dropped back onto the couch. When her vision cleared again, she got back up and successfully walked into the kitchen.

She hadn't planned to walk into the kitchen. It was simply where her legs took her. She walked over to one of the drawers and pulled it open.

Allison had plenty of knives in there.

She had at least a half-dozen that would do the trick. She knew where to cut—she wouldn't do it across the wrists, like an amateur.

She picked up one of them. The sharpest. Made in Japan. It even had a Japanese symbol on the blade, though she didn't know what it meant.

Allison put the knife back in the drawer without touching it to her flesh. She tried to tell herself that she was doing it for Spiral, because the cat needed somebody to care for it, even a monster like her, but she was doing it for herself. She didn't want to die, even if she deserved to be removed from the world.

She had no idea what to do.

She knew where the couple lived. She could find them by waiting outside of their building, or by going door to door until she found the right apartment. But what could she do? What could she say? He'd mentioned their financial woes, but what was she going to do, try to pay them off for their tragic loss? "*Sorry I killed your baby. What's your PayPal address?*"

They probably didn't want to see her.

Was Daxton calling the police? Was he vowing to never speak of what had happened, since it couldn't possibly be real? Was he driving home to grab a shotgun?

Allison hated the idea of being reactive, but that seemed like the smartest approach. Try to get herself under control as she waited to see what happened. If he returned, maybe they could discuss things in a much calmer manner.

At least she hadn't killed him.

God, what if she'd broken his neck? The woman would've lost her baby *and* her baby's father, all because of her.

Allison went into her bedroom and changed out of her sweatpants and into a pair of jeans. She'd message Jamison and tell him she needed the rest of the day off. Then maybe she'd walk around outside, staying close enough to the house that she could hear a car approach, and try to work through the horror and the self-loathing.

AFTER ALMOST DRIVING off the road twice, Daxton pulled off to the side so that he could compose himself.

The bruises had mostly faded from his beating two weeks ago, so he wasn't happy that a whole new set would replace them, but his real concern right now was: *what the fuck had happened?*

He hadn't simply imagined her flinging him across the room. Even when he occasionally indulged in a mind-altering substance —which he hadn't since Maggie got knocked up—he wouldn't hallucinate something like that. If he truly, desperately needed to come up with a logical real-world-physics explanation, the best he could do was guess that she'd set some sort of trap with clear fishing line, which yanked him across the room and into the wall. That explanation was so stupid that he was going with the paranormal one.

That bitch had flung him across the room without touching him.

She hadn't *wanted* to do it. In fact, she'd actively tried to get him to leave.

Suddenly her behavior outside their apartment building made more sense. Instead of being happy that she'd stopped Maggie from falling, she'd been worried that she'd harmed the baby with her...telepathic powers? No, telepathic was like ESP. Tele-something. It didn't matter.

A woman who could do something like that might be pretty damn useful.

This could be the opportunity to get himself back in Winlaw's good graces.

Daxton took out his phone and made a call.

8

"I need help with a kidnapping," Daxton told Mick over the phone. They'd worked together on a few jobs. He was a reliable guy. "There aren't any neighbors, so we don't have to worry about that part, but we have to do it quick. Break in, grab her, and get out."

"Did you clear this with Winlaw?"

"I'm delivering her to him, but he wouldn't understand if I tried to explain it to him now. I need to take her someplace secure and verify some stuff first."

"I don't know," said Mick. "That could bring a lot of heat. It needs to go through Winlaw."

"There's no heat. She's a nobody. We're not starting any kind of gang war. It's just a bizarre situation and I need to make sure I can explain it correctly. You have my word, Winlaw will be *delighted* with the end product, but I can't bring him into the loop quite yet."

"Winlaw isn't delighted very often."

"I hear that, believe me. Trust me on this one. If I try to tell him about it, he'll say that I'm out of my mind, but once I show him what she can do, I'll be golden. We'll both be golden."

"What can she do?"

"Seriously, you just have to trust me on this one. Are you in?"

"Yeah, I'm in."

"Do you have Chloroform? Or do you have tranquilizer darts? That would be even better."

"I'll see what I can dig up."

"Perfect, thank you." Daxton gave him the address and hung up. Then he called Maggie.

"How'd it go?" she asked.

"I didn't get any money out of her, but it might be even better than we thought. I'll explain everything later. It's gonna be good."

"How did she react?"

"You said you didn't want the details."

"I know. Just give me...you're right, I don't want to know. Give me the high level version."

"She wasn't happy."

"How upset was she?" Maggie asked.

"Look, either you want to be shielded from it or you don't. I'll tell you what's going on later. I'm not sure when I'll be home."

"All right. Be careful."

"I always am."

Daxton hung up. He rotated his shoulder, which was really sore but didn't seem to be seriously injured. He obviously couldn't bring Allison to his apartment, but there were a couple of places he could store her. He'd get the evidence of her abilities on video, then present it to Mr. Winlaw. Boom! Redemption!

His phone rang. Winlaw. *Shit.*

"This is Daxton," he said.

"Are you a fucking idiot?" Winlaw asked.

Daxton immediately broke into a cold sweat. "No, sir."

"I just spoke with Mick. When people who work for me are asked to keep secrets from me, the smart and loyal ones know to report that immediately. Unless I'm remembering incorrectly, we had a bit of a problem not too long ago. Surely you would not be so stupid as to risk enraging me when you're already on the thinnest ice imaginable."

Daxton hoped he at least lived long enough to kill Mick. "Sir, please, I swear to God that I wasn't trying to screw you over. It's completely the opposite. I just—I just had this opportunity come up, one that could make you lots of money, but I didn't want to come to you until I knew exactly what I had to offer."

"Sounds like bullshit."

"It's not. I swear it's not. You can't honestly believe that I'd try to screw you over right now."

"It completely defies credibility," said Winlaw. "So imagine my surprise to have Mick call to say that you'd asked him to keep a secret from me, and imagine my further surprise that you haven't denied it."

"There's this lady," Daxton said, trying to keep his voice steady. "She could be valuable."

"Valuable how?"

What the hell was Daxton supposed to say? That she had magic powers? That would enrage Winlaw even further. Daxton needed to be able to *prove* what Allison could do before he handed her over.

Think! C'mon, think!

"She came into a lot of money. From a bank job about a decade ago. With proper motivation, I'm sure she'll say where the cash is hidden."

"And you were going to share this with me?"

"Yes! Of course!"

"You know somebody who can tell you where a very large sum of money is hidden, and you were going to kidnap her to make her reveal this information, and even though you told Mick not to tell me about it, you had every intention of sharing this big score with me. Am I understanding correctly?"

Fuck! That had been a terrible cover story. What had he been thinking?

He needed to call Maggie immediately. Tell her to run. Winlaw might have already sent his goons after her.

"Mr. Winlaw—"

"Enough. You're insulting my intelligence. This is going to be horrible for you, Daxton. Do you know the sensation you're feeling right now? The one where your body *isn't* consumed with unbearable, excruciating agony? Don't get used to it. I'm not a skilled enough wordsmith to describe just how awful the end of your life is going to be, so use your imagination. Go ahead and run. It'll be that much more satisfying when we catch you."

Daxton's hand was perspiring so heavily that he almost dropped the phone. "It's not like that at all. It's not. I'll come clean, okay? I'll tell you exactly what happened."

"I'm listening."

"This lady, she threw me across her living room without

touching me. I swear it's true. I *swear* it's true. I wouldn't make something like this up. I flew ten, twelve feet across the room and smashed into the wall. She's tele-something. I don't know the word."

"Telekinetic?"

"Yes! That!"

"You should have stuck with the other story," said Winlaw.

"No, no, no, no, no, it's true. I knew you wouldn't believe me. You *shouldn't* believe me. Nobody should believe me. That's why I needed to kidnap her first. So I could prove it. So you wouldn't think I was insulting your intelligence. It's true. Send Mick out here. I'm not running anywhere. We'll catch her, we'll bring her someplace safe, and I'll prove it. I'm not trying to scam you. Send Mick. I'll prove it, you'll see."

"You're telling me that you have a telekinetic woman, and your plan was to kidnap her, and deliver her to me?"

"Yes! Exactly! A woman who can do that, who knows how valuable she'd be to you? Who knows what else she can do?"

"Congratulations, Daxton. You've captured my interest."

"Thank you. Thank you, sir."

"I was going to leave Maggie out of this. I'm not in the habit of torturing pregnant women to death. If you're lying to me, if you make a run for it, you will watch her suffer an unimaginable fate before something even worse happens to you. I mean *unimaginable*. I'll have to do it myself, because I can't pay anybody enough to make it worth living with the memory of what they've done."

Daxton totally believed him.

"So," Winlaw continued, "I'm going to give you the chance to keep her out of it and admit that you were trying to pull one over on me. If you want to stick to the telekinetic woman story, your girlfriend becomes fully involved. What's your decision?"

"I'm telling you the truth," Daxton insisted.

"All right. Then I'm going to give you the benefit of the doubt."

"Thank you."

"I don't believe for one second that you're going to kidnap a woman with telekinetic abilities, but I'll be interested to see what you do deliver to me."

"You'll be impressed, I promise." It was entirely possible that Allison would refuse to demonstrate her abilities no matter how many blades he jammed underneath her fingernails, or that she simply couldn't perform on command, but Daxton wouldn't worry about that right now.

"We'll see."

Daxton didn't want to work with that asshole Mick, even if he'd been driven purely by self-preservation. "This isn't a one-person job. It's okay for me to call somebody to help out, right?"

"I'll send Forrest to assist you," said Winlaw.

"*Forrest?* No."

"After all this, you think you have a choice?"

"Come on, Mr. Winlaw. Why him?"

"Forrest is excellent at what he does."

"He's creepy as hell," said Daxton. "It skeeves me out to be around him. I have to take a shower afterward."

"Oh my goodness gracious, I'm so very sorry that he makes you uncomfortable. He's nearby and I trust him. If you'd come to me in the first place, you could have your pick of partners."

"Anybody but Forrest. Literally anybody else will be fine. He'll fuck it up just by being himself."

"I'd like you to stop arguing with me now, Daxton."

"All right. Fine. Send Forrest. The address is—"

"Mick already gave me the address."

"Of course he did."

"Stay put. Forrest will be there soon." Winlaw hung up.

Daxton wiped his forehead. It wasn't just his hands—his entire body was drenched in sweat. This was too much at once. The mind wasn't designed to cope with proof of the supernatural and Winlaw's anger so close to each other.

He'd be okay. This would work out. It had to.

He'd make sure Forrest understood that this wasn't a normal kidnapping victim, and they'd move with maximum efficiency.

He turned the car back around so he could keep an eye on Allison's house while he waited.

9

Allison paced around the house. Her home was suffocating her, but she didn't want to leave until Jamison had given his okay for her to take the rest of the day off. So she just walked quickly from room to room, occasionally glancing at her work computer to see if he'd responded yet.

She wished she could talk to somebody about this.

Cody knew her secret and he'd witnessed the whole thing. But their new friendship had formed when they thought everything was going to be all right. Allison had managed to convince herself that the baby was fine. If she confessed to him that she had, in fact, killed the woman's unborn child, he wouldn't lend a sympathetic ear. He'd be horrified. Outraged. As he should be.

So all she could do right now was quickly walk around her house, trying to withstand the urge to start screaming and tearing out her hair. Trying to keep it together, in case the father-not-to-be returned with the police.

She could make it through this. She'd made it through worse.

ALLISON SAT ON THE BED, her back against the wall, staring at the open doorway as if expecting one of the corpses in the cabin to walk past. None of them did. She'd been sitting here all night, and Mom, Dad, and the two dead men remained silent and unseen.

Her need to pee was almost unbearable at this point. And she knew she had to go out there eventually. If she covered her eyes, she might trip over a corpse, so she'd have to look at what she'd done.

She wished she could believe that it was all a figment of her imagination. The men hadn't showed up to rob them. She hadn't killed them. She hadn't killed Mom and Dad. Mom was happily painting, and Dad was happily reading, and Allison had gotten so carried away with the drawing she was making that she thought it was real life. She wished she could believe that. She wished she could believe that she'd been sitting on this bed all night—the sun was rising now—for no good reason, because everything was perfectly normal in the rest of the cabin. She wished she were younger. More childish. Six years old. Maybe eight. Not ten. A ten-year-old was too old to live in a fantasy world and believe that her parents were still alive.

Allison got off the bed and carefully tiptoed into the main room of the cabin.

The four dead bodies were still there, broken and bloody.

She hurried out of the cabin and ran to the outhouse.

She stayed in there for a long time after she was done. Finally, she decided that she couldn't live in the outhouse forever, and stepped outside.

It was a beautiful day. The sun was shining.

That was bad. Dead bodies didn't do well in the sun.

Allison had no idea what to do. She could find another cabin and get help. Or, at the very least, she could walk to the car. It would only take about ten minutes. She'd never driven a car but she understood the basics and was sure she could figure it out. It wouldn't be difficult for her to get help and bring the police to the cabin.

What would she tell them?

What if they figured out that it was her fault?

What if they took her to a laboratory? Studied her. Drew blood. Sliced off parts of her and peered at them through a microscope.

Or took her to prison. No, not prison—juvenile hall. She didn't know what life was like for a murderous ten-year-old girl in there, but it had to be a nightmare.

They wouldn't know she did it unless she told them.

But how would she explain it? How would she explain four dead bodies to the police? Bodies with broken arms and legs and ribs and necks. How had they gotten that way?

If she was willing to use one of the guns, she could make it look like the men had shot Mom and Dad. Maybe the broken bones had happened when the four of them fought.

No. Even if she *was* willing to do that, they'd know that Mom and Dad been shot long after they were dead. Allison didn't understand how the science worked on that, but she knew they could figure it out. They had experts.

She could just say that she didn't know what happened. She'd heard screams and been too scared to come out of the room. When she finally did, everybody was dead.

She was a ten-year-old girl. Big for her age, sure, but still a ten-year-old girl. They wouldn't think she was a killer.

But she was a terrible liar. And they had tests. They'd know.

They might not even believe her if she told the truth. They might actually lock her up with the crazy people if she tried to say that she killed them with her mind.

She just didn't know what to do.

Hide the bodies? Bury them?

Tell the police that Mom and Dad had gone for a walk and never came back?

She'd have to drag the bodies deep into the woods. It would take a really long time. Days, maybe. Digging graves would take even longer. And she'd have to go back and cover the trail she made.

She'd miss something.

They'd find where she buried the bodies.

Find a piece of her fingernail in the dirt.

Things would be much worse for her than they already were.

She'd have to just leave things the way they were. It was too risky to do otherwise. She'd just swear that she didn't know what happened, and pray that they didn't suspect she had anything to do with it.

What if she accidentally murdered a police officer?

She'd killed Mom and Dad without meaning to. It could

happen again. Who knew how upset she might get if they started interrogating her?

But what could she do about it? Run and hide away forever?

The best thing she could do was make up a story, stick to it no matter what, and hope that the truth was so insane that nobody would ever suspect it.

Allison didn't want to go back into the cabin, but she needed the car keys. She knew where they were: on the table next to the lamp. Thank God they weren't in Dad's pocket.

As she walked inside, she glanced over at her mother, who barely looked like Mom anymore. Her face was twisted, her jaw broken. Her eyes were open.

Allison grabbed the keys and hurried back outside.

She took the wrong trail at first and had to backtrack. On the right trail, she had to stop to rest a couple of times because it was so hard for her to breathe. But finally she reached the car. She got it started with no problem. Actually driving it was a challenge because she wasn't tall enough to reach the gas pedal and completely see over the dashboard, so she had to drive by flooring the accelerator and then steering while the car coasted. She somehow managed to make it all the way along the narrow dirt road without crashing or getting stuck.

When she reached the paved road, she did okay for a minute or two, until a car behind her, annoyed at her slow speed, blasted its horn and made her go off the road. The driver, shocked to see a ten-year-old girl behind the wheel, drove her to the nearest police station, where she completely broke down and wasn't able to speak for a long time.

"Can you tell us what happened?"

The police officer was nice, or at least pretended to be. She had a pretty smile.

Allison shrugged. She'd planned out exactly what she was going to say, but thought it would be better if they had to drag it out of her.

She had left the door open and animals had gotten into the cabin. They'd eaten part of the bodies—at least that's what Allison had overheard. She didn't know how bad it was. She was seated in the front seat of the police car, which should have been exciting but wasn't exciting at all.

"Take your time, sweetie," said the police officer.

"Somebody knocked on the door," said Allison. "Dad answered, and these two guys came in. They pointed guns at us."

"Did they say what they wanted?"

"They wanted money. Dad gave them some, and Mom and Dad gave them their rings, but it wasn't enough. They got mad. Mom made me go into the bedroom and shut the door and promise not to come out. Then I just heard screaming."

The police officer nodded. "Your mother and father screaming?"

"Everybody screaming."

"And what did you do?"

Allison lowered her eyes. "I stayed in the room."

"For how long?"

"Until the screaming stopped. I don't know how long it was."

"And then what did you do?"

"I ran out of the cabin and went to get the car. But it was dark outside and I got lost. I slept by a tree. In the morning I found the car and tried to drive for help. I went off the road but a man gave me a ride to see the police."

"Is there anything else you can tell me, Allison? Anything at all?"

"No."

"Okay."

"Do you know what happened to them?"

"We don't," said the police officer. "Not yet. We're still trying to piece it together. I'm going to take you to the station and we'll get you something to eat. We'll probably ask you some more questions. Is that all right?"

"Yes."

"You're being really brave. I know it's sad and scary, but we'll take care of you. You're going to be okay."

ALLISON DIDN'T KNOW how the investigation had turned out. The bones, broken from the inside, wouldn't match injuries from something like a baseball bat, so the coroner was probably at a loss for what had occurred. Even if the injuries had been from an external source, nobody would've believed that a ten-year-old girl could beat four adults to death. The final report certainly didn't say, "*Probable supernatural cause. Check daughter for paranormal abilities.*" In the end, she was an orphan but not a prisoner or a lab rat.

She walked back into her office. Her instant messenger alert was flashing. Jamison said that it was absolutely no problem to take the rest of the day off, and that he hoped she'd feel better soon.

A long walk—a *really* long walk—would help her calm down.

She picked up her phone and saw that she had a text from Cody. *How's everything going?*

She texted back: *ok.*

That doesn't sound okay. Do you want to talk?

Aren't you at work?

I'll take a break.

I don't want to get you in trouble.

They allow me to take breaks. It's required by law. How about I call you in a couple of minutes?

Okay, Allison texted, even though she had specifically decided that she would not confide in Cody. Her texting fingers and her brain were not communicating properly.

Cell phone reception was probably fine in the woods behind her house, but she didn't want to be distracted when she was walking over uneven terrain, so she just paced around the house for a couple of minutes until he called.

"Hi," she answered.

"Hi. I'm here to offer my amazing listening services."

"I don't really have anything to say."

"Are you sure?" Cody asked.

"No."

"I know we only met yesterday, but it's okay to tell me stuff, I promise. Everything you say will be a total secret. I won't betray your trust."

"The father came over to my house."

"Uninvited?"

"Yeah."

"What did he want?"

"She lost the baby."

"Oh, shit. Allison, I'm sorry."

"Don't feel sorry for me. I'm the bad guy."

"No, you're not. I feel sorry for them, too, but you're not the bad guy. Did they say exactly what happened?"

"She went to the emergency room, and then she had a miscarriage. If I'd just let her fall, she would've been better off."

"Are they sure it was because of you?"

"*I'm* sure it was because of me."

"Right, but...I don't want to be too graphic, but do they know...I mean, was there proof?"

"I didn't demand to inspect the fetus, if that's what you're asking."

"No, no, that's not what I meant," said Cody. "I just don't want you blaming yourself if you're not sure."

"I'm sure."

"Okay."

"You can hang up now."

"My break isn't over."

"That's not what I meant."

"If you're hoping that I'll start treating you like Satan, you're going to be very disappointed. It wasn't your fault. Or maybe it was your fault, but it was still an accident. I mean, they have those Good Samaritan laws for a reason. Nobody is going to say that you should have let a pregnant woman fall down the stairs. You reacted the way any decent human being would react."

"No, a decent human being, knowing what she was capable of, would not have put herself in that situation."

"Can we talk in person?" Cody asked.

"No. I'm really upset. It wouldn't be safe."

"What if I came over, and we talked on the phone but stayed a safe distance away from each other?"

"What good would that do?"

"We could look at each other. It's a nice way to talk."

"I was going for a walk."

"That's fine. I can't leave right away. I'll come over after work."

"I don't think it's a good idea," Allison said.

"I think it's a great idea."

"It's not."

"I feel like you could really use a friend right now. Somebody that you can see."

"Are you worried that I'll do something stupid?"

"Stupid isn't the word I'd use, but I do feel like it's a good idea for somebody to keep an eye on you, even if it's from afar."

"Fine," Allison said. "I'll text you my address. What time do you get off work?"

"Four."

It wasn't even ten o'clock yet. "Okay. Let me know when you're on your way. I guess I'll have you park at the end of the driveway and not get out of your car."

"Looking forward to seeing you again. I'm sorry this happened."

"Me too."

Allison hung up. She'd look at him through her living room window, and if she felt her anxiety level start to rise, she'd send him away.

She shoved the phone into her pocket, then went out the back door, hoping that some fresh air would make her feel less like a monster.

10

From his vantage point, with binoculars, Daxton could see Allison walk into her backyard. She was walking quickly but not running, and she wasn't carrying anything.

She went into the woods behind her house, seemingly unaware that he was watching her.

That was fine. Maybe she was just going for a walk. If she was trying to flee, she'd at least take a purse, right? If she'd sprinted outside immediately after he'd left, that would make sense, but half an hour later, she wouldn't make a run for it empty-handed. This was nothing to worry about.

A few minutes later, a car pulled up behind him. He'd hoped that maybe Forrest was unavailable and that Winlaw would send somebody else, but nope, it was that big creepy fucker. He got out of his own car, walked over to the passenger-side front door of Daxton's car, and rapped his knuckles on the glass. Daxton gestured for him to get inside.

As Forrest opened the door, before he'd even slid into the seat, Daxton smelled his overpowering odor. He smelled like he'd had nasty sex two days ago and never showered. He pulled the lever to scoot the seat back, then closed the door.

"Hey," he said. Forrest had a surprisingly high and squeaky voice for such a big, bulky guy. His blond hair was cut military-short, with several patches of dandruff visible on his scalp.

"Did you bring Chloroform?"

"Yeah. And a rag. Not a clean one." He chuckled.

"You're going to follow my lead on this," Daxton told him. "I'm in charge."

Forrest laughed. He had a yellow glob on his front tooth. "Damn, at least let me get settled before you start barking orders at me."

"I wasn't barking an order. I was explaining how this is gonna work."

"Well, Daxie, from what I understand you're not really in a position to be on a power trip. I hear you messed up but good. I hear your testicles are in danger of being slit open and unspooled." He leaned over, speaking to Daxton's crotch. "Is that true, little testes? Are you in danger?"

"Knock it off. This is a dangerous job and you'd better take it seriously."

"How dangerous can it be? It's one girl."

"I wouldn't have asked for help if it was an easy job. She's mentally ill. She might be heavily armed."

"I hope she is. Chicks with guns turn me on so bad. Might pop a chub while we're in there."

"See, this is why I didn't want you here. You're not taking this seriously."

"You didn't want me here?"

"Fuck no."

Forrest chuckled. "That's hurtful."

"I mean it, I'm in charge. You'll do exactly what I say."

"You're the boss. At least until the boss tortures you to death."

"Funny."

"If you want to see it as funny, that's fine with me." Forrest checked his fingernails, which were in desperate need of clipping and cleaning. He stuck his thumb under his front teeth and ran it back and forth.

"She's not home right now," said Daxton. "She went out for a walk in the woods behind her house. We'll grab her when she gets back."

"Why not just go after her in the woods?"

"It's an uncontrolled environment. She'd see or hear us coming and she'd know she was in danger. I can still knock on her door under the guise that I want to have a conversation."

"Who cares if she knows she's in danger? You don't think we can catch her?"

"What if she calls 911?"

"Think she can do that while she's sprinting through the woods? I'm pretty damn fast. If she tries to make a phone call while I'm chasing her, she's going to fall and smash her face open."

"We're not following her into the woods."

Forrest shrugged. "You're the boss."

"We're not in a rush here. If you have somewhere to be, by all means go keep your appointment. You won't hurt my feelings."

"I have nowhere else to be. I wouldn't want to deprive you of my company." He scraped underneath his thumbnail with his front teeth again. "So why are you kidnapping this lady?"

"That's on a need-to-know basis, and you don't need to know."

"Is it revenge?"

"I just said you don't need to know."

"But you think she'll let us in for a conversation?"

"She sure as hell won't let you in, because you're the kind of creepy motherfucker that smart people don't let into their homes. She may not let me in, either. But we'll get in."

"Yeah, we will," said Forrest. "She can't keep us out. We'll kick that door down and make her suffer."

"Whatever."

"Why do you think she might not let you in?"

Daxton figured he should give Forrest that information, in case it came up during the actual kidnapping. "She believes that she killed my kid."

"You have a kid?"

"On the way."

"Shit. Maggie lost the baby?"

Daxton hated hearing Forrest say her name. "No. The baby's fine. But the lady thinks she was responsible for a miscarriage, and I was going to try to squeeze some money out of her for it."

"Wow," said Forrest. "That is *dark*."

"I like to seize opportunities."

"But the baby's okay?"

"Yes. I just said that."

"I understand. I wanted to make sure I heard correctly." Forrest licked his lips. "Have you ever killed a baby?"

"No."

"It's really something."

"I'm sure it is."

"It's actually not about the baby. The baby isn't putting up a fight or posing any kind of challenge. It's all about the mother's reaction."

"I don't want to hear about it," said Daxton.

"And I don't want to talk about it. The memory is just for me."

"I need you to stop talking. Just sit there and don't say a word, okay?"

"That's fine," said Forrest. "I've got plenty to think about."

They sat in the car, silent except for Forrest's heavy breathing.

As SHE WALKED through the woods, Allison came up with a plan.

She'd anonymously pay their medical bills. Or what she could afford. She wasn't rich by any stretch of the imagination, but she had some savings. It would help ease her conscience without looking like an offensive attempt to pay off their sorrow with a check.

She wasn't sure what she'd do if Daxton came back. It would depend on how he confronted her about what happened. She couldn't imagine that she'd confess the way she did with Cody, but she didn't like the idea of gaslighting somebody she'd flung across the room in that way. She'd see how antagonistic he was if he returned. Most likely, he wouldn't come back. He'd already delivered the news and there was nothing more to say.

If he returned with the cops, she would calmly lie. Yes, she'd stopped his girlfriend from falling down the stairs. Yes, she'd been emotional about it. No, of course she hadn't thrown him across the room. Did she look strong enough to do something like that? Seriously, he claimed she did it without even touching him? How was she supposed to react to something so ridiculous? He was clearly impacted by the tragedy, and she absolutely didn't blame him, but they had to keep a grip on objective reality here, right?

In theory, the authorities would laugh off his story before they even agreed to pay her a visit. And Allison couldn't allow herself to be aggressively interrogated. Locked in a room with a cop across the desk, stressed out of her mind...bad things would happen.

She didn't even know if that was how they'd question her. It could be much less formal and much less intimidating. Still, she could not be in a high-pressure situation like that, or her predicament would become so much worse.

She stepped out of the woods into her backyard. She didn't feel a lot better, but this had helped a little, so it had been a good use of forty-five minutes. Hopefully the "pay off their hospital bill" idea would work without further conflict.

"SHE'S BACK," said Daxton.

Forrest cracked his knuckles. "Good. Let's do this."

"No. We have to give it at least ten more minutes."

"Why?"

"Because if we walk right up to the door as soon as she goes back into the house, she'll know we were watching her."

"Are you scared of her?" Forrest asked.

"I'm scared of you being reckless."

"You know me. I like to keep things light beforehand, but once we start, I'm all business. When I'm on a job, it goes well. No dead kids."

"He wasn't a kid," said Daxton. "He was a full-grown adult who should've known what he was doing."

"Oh, I didn't mean Winlaw's son-in-law. I would never bring that up. That would be tactless. I was talking about actual dead kids. The job I was referring to went horribly. I should've been there to keep everything on a professional level."

"I thought we'd agreed not to talk."

"You're the one who started talking."

"Well, let's stop."

Forrest shrugged and cracked his knuckles again.

ALLISON ALMOST WANTED to text Cody to tell him not to come over. Now that she was a little calmer, the idea of talking to him on her cell phone while he sat at the end of the driveway seemed like a really awful second date. Why call extra attention to the fact that she could accidentally murder the people she cared about?

For now she wouldn't dissuade him. She had a few hours to decide what she wanted.

She went inside through the back door and walked into her living room. She sat down on the couch next to Spiral, who immediately crawled onto her lap and began to purr.

Allison was exhausted. A nap held great appeal right now.

No. If she took a nap now she'd regret it tonight. She had a remarkable ability to be unbearably tired all day and then wide-awake the instant she hit the pillow. It would be worse tonight. No sense compounding the problem even further with a nap.

She'd just sit here and pet her cat. Purring made everything better.

"ALL RIGHT," said Daxton. "Let's go. Where's the Chloroform?"

"In my car."

"Get it."

"I know. We're not going to leave without your precious Chloroform. Have you ever tried knocking yourself out with it?"

"I said, let's go." Daxton got out of his car. Forrest got out, walked over to his own car, and retrieved a small brown paper bag.

"I've got my knock-out juice, I've got my gun, and I've got my knife. Anything else?"

"Leave the gun."

"That's not going to happen."

"We're delivering her to Winlaw. We're not killing her."

"I understand that. But I'm not putting myself into a potentially dangerous situation without my gun. I can tell that you're carrying."

"I know I won't shoot her. I don't trust you."

Forrest chuckled. "I'm well aware that you don't like me, but Winlaw sent me for a reason. You, Daxie, are the one who's trying to redeem himself. I'm totally good. If I screw this up, maybe Winlaw will try to Kirkwood me, but that's not your problem. So who does Daxton Sink worry about?"

"Shut the fuck up."

"I'll ask again. Who does Daxton Sink worry about?"

"I said, shut the fuck up."

"He worries about Daxton Sink, that's who. Don't worry about me. I've got this. Now let's go slam a Chloroform-soaked rag into that bitch's face."

Daxton and Forrest walked toward the house. Daxton wouldn't take all of the blame if this job went bad, but he couldn't be part of two disasters in a row, even if Forrest was the one who botched it. But Forrest, repulsive as he was, knew what he was doing. This would go fine.

"Here's how it's going to work," Daxton said. "I'm going to knock on the front door while you pick the lock in the back. If you even have to—maybe she leaves the door unlocked when she's home. I'll keep her distracted. You sneak in, get as close as you can without her noticing, and then pounce with the rag."

Forrest nodded. "Not very elegant, but I like it."

"Just get her with the rag. Don't hurt her."

"I'm not going to start biting her fingers off. I will ever so gently lower her unconscious form to the floor, taking care to get nary a hair out of place."

"I know you're trying to be an asshole, but that's the right way to do this. I'm trusting you."

Forrest gave him a salute, then hurried around the back of the house.

Daxton walked up onto the front porch and rang the doorbell.

11

Allison opened the door but didn't unfasten the chain lock. Oh, God. It was him.

"I'm not here to cause any problems," Daxton said, holding up his hands. "I'm here to apologize."

"Why would you need to apologize?"

"Because you don't just show up at somebody's house and burden them with that kind of thing. That was horrible of me. There's no excuse for that, no matter how bad things are in my life. Your reaction was completely understandable."

"My reaction?"

"Screaming at me. Hitting me so that I smacked into the wall. I'm not trying to sound insincere here—I'm not saying it was the *right* thing to do, just that I understand it. It was a tense moment."

"Yes," said Allison. "It was."

Did Daxton really believe that she'd hit him? Was it possible that, playing it back in his memory, this was the only explanation that made sense?

"May I come in for a couple of minutes?" he asked. "I'm not going to take up much of your time. I have to get back to the hospital. I'd just like to apologize so that we can leave things in a better place."

"Of course," said Allison, unfastening the chain lock. She opened the door and Daxton walked inside.

"Thank you," he said.

"Can I get you something to drink?"

"Oh, no. I'm not here to impose."

"It's no problem at all."

"No, no. I'm fine, really. I feel like I may have implied that you were to blame for what happened, and nothing could be further from the truth. I apologize if I chose my words badly. I've been under a lot of stress, but that's no excuse."

"You didn't say anything wrong," Allison told him.

"It's kind of you to say that, but we both know it's not true. So let me be perfectly clear: this was not your fault, we do not blame you in any way, and you should feel no responsibility."

"I appreciate that. But I'd like to help out with the medical bills."

"That's not necessary. I would never ask that of you."

"You didn't ask. I'm offering."

"No," said Daxton. "You do a good deed and have to pay for it? That wouldn't be right. It goes against the idea that this absolutely wasn't your fault, and it's not at all why I came back. I just wanted to apologize, give you a hug, and let you know that everything is going to be all right."

Allison had been feeling an intense, almost overwhelming

sense of relief. When he held out his arms for a hug, the vibe changed a bit. It wasn't simply that Allison wasn't a hugger. Daxton had a subtle change in demeanor, a sudden sense of desperation, as if he knew he was trying too hard. She'd believed everything he said up until this point, but in this moment she worried that he hadn't only come back to apologize.

"I'm sorry," she said. "I'm not much of a hugger."

He lowered his arms. "Neither am I. I just thought it was appropriate here."

"Will you settle for a handshake?"

"Of course."

He stepped forward, staring into her eyes. Staring too intensely into her eyes, as if he was purposely trying not to break eye contact.

Allison did not consider herself a particularly good judge of character, but she could tell when something felt *wrong*, and if her powers had included something useful like Spidey Sense, it would be tingling right now.

She glanced behind her.

There was another man in the house.

He was about ten feet away. A big, scary looking guy holding a dripping rag.

He lunged at her.

Allison screamed.

Forrest, with that creepy-ass grin, rushed at Allison as soon as she saw him. Daxton had a moment of horror, thinking that he'd grab her, snap her neck, and say "Oops," as her dead body dropped to the floor.

Instead, right before he reached her, he just stopped.

His outstretched arms fell to his sides. He dropped the Chloroform-soaked rag to the floor.

Forrest stood there, looking bewildered.

Daxton should have used this opportunity to grab Allison from behind. Drag her over to the rag and shove her face into it. Instead, he took a great big step back.

Now Forrest looked like he had an instant migraine.

His mouth fell open but he didn't say anything.

His whole body began to quiver.

Tackle her, Daxton thought, but he couldn't bring himself to do it. He didn't want her to focus her attention on him. He wanted Forrest, who was bigger and stronger, to break free of whatever spell she had over him and take her out.

Daxton had a goddamn gun. He could threaten her with it. He could make her stop.

But he wasn't prepared to actually shoot her. And if she called his bluff…

Basically, he was a fucking coward. Her display of power had terrified him and he couldn't bring himself to attack her for fear of getting a second dose of it.

Forrest gave him a pleading look, as if mentally begging for help.

Thin rivulets of blood trickled down the sides of his mouth.

Daxton took another big step backwards.

Forrest whimpered. Daxton didn't know if it was from terror, excruciating pain, or both.

Do something, for God's sake!

Forrest's whimper turned into a moan. A bloody tooth dropped out of his mouth. Then another.

Blood ran down his lips and from his nostrils, as teeth kept falling to the floor.

His eyes went wide and he started to gasp for breath, as if choking on a molar.

He coughed, sending a spray of six or seven teeth into the air.

Blood began to stream down his face from his ears.

At this point, Daxton knew he had to get the hell out of there. But there was still Winlaw's rage to contend with, so he couldn't just flee the house, run to his car, and speed off.

Forrest dropped to his knees. Blood was now leaking from his eyes. The poor bastard was still alive but that wasn't going to last much longer. More teeth fell out of his mouth. As soon as he died, Allison would almost certainly come after Daxton, so he needed to figure out a plan, immediately.

Just get her!

No. He couldn't do it.

Shoot her in the leg!

Shooting her in the leg might solve the problem, and it might mean that seconds later he had blood gushing from all of his orifices.

Then he saw her cell phone resting on the coffee table.

He'd swipe it and run. Trap her in the house without a way to call for help.

Without further thought, he rushed for the phone and grabbed it. Forrest let out a cry of agony as Daxton ran for the front door. He threw the door open, hurried outside, and pulled it shut.

He took out his pocketknife and frantically ran around the house, looking for a cable. There it was. He cut the white cord, hoping this would kill her Internet access. He ran around the rest of the house, but didn't see any other cables.

Then, because he didn't know how far her homicidal powers could reach, he fled from her yard.

THERE WAS a loud *crack* as either the man's neck broke or his skull did.

He flopped forward onto the carpet and lay still.

Allison stumbled backwards, hands over her mouth.

She couldn't panic. Daxton, though he'd run from the house, was still a problem. She needed to go after him. She hoped she could finish this without killing him—maybe she'd be able to just break his leg—but she wasn't going to let him get away.

She opened the front door and stepped outside.

Daxton, who was at the edge of her yard, stopped running and spun around to face her. He reached under his shirt and took out a gun.

Allison quickly stepped back inside and pulled the door closed.

She glanced around for her phone. It wasn't on the coffee table where she'd left it, and she was pretty sure Daxton had taken it while she was focused on his friend. She didn't have a landline, but there had to be a website for 911, right?

She hurried into her office and pressed the escape key to take her work laptop out of hibernation mode. No Internet connection. She clicked on the icon to pull up the list of wireless networks in the area, but "Allison T" was missing and the other two were both password protected.

She peeked out the side window, hoping that Daxton had continued running. But he was in the same spot, a cell phone to his ear. She gazed at him through the glass, staring as hard as she could, trying to envision blood gushing out of his eye sockets.

Nothing happened.

From where he stood, he'd be able to see her if she went out the back door. She might be able to race into the woods without him shooting her. She might not. She had no idea how good of a shot Daxton was. For now, it seemed like more of a risk than just staying put.

The windows on the other side of the house were painted shut. He'd hear if she tried to break them. And she couldn't control her powers well enough to know for sure that she stood a chance against a gun-wielding psycho pursuing her through the woods.

She returned to her living room. A pool of blood was expanding around the dead man's body. Spiral stood there, poking at it with his front paw, so she picked the cat up and put him back on the couch.

She went into the kitchen and took down four pots. She filled each of them with water and placed them on the stove, setting each burner on high. Then she opened the drawer where she kept her knives. She had six or seven good ones, including a butcher knife, and she set them out on the counter. Allison took the butcher knife with her as she peeked out the window to check on Daxton.

He was still there.

Was there a way to reason with him? Negotiate?

Probably not.

She concentrated on him again, envisioning his legs shattering beneath him, the bones breaking into a million shards. She even tried gesturing with her hands, as if practicing witchcraft, but it had no effect.

She couldn't hurt him from here, but he couldn't hurt her from there.

Though she'd watch for an opportunity to escape, if he brought the fight back to her, she'd be ready to destroy him.

12

"Forrest is dead!" Daxton blurted into the phone as soon as Winlaw answered. "She killed him just by looking at him!"

"Calm down," said Winlaw. "Explain to me exactly what happened."

"I'm not going to calm down! He came up behind her, and when she looked at him his goddamn teeth started to fall out of his mouth! There was blood coming from everywhere! She killed him without even doing anything!"

"Are you trying to scam me, Daxton?"

"No! I need you to send more men! Send a dozen! Send them all at once! Get them here as soon as you can!"

"I can't get you a dozen men."

"Get as many as you can. Right now. As far as I know, I cut off her communication, but I can't keep her trapped in the house forever. Think of what you could do if you had somebody like her under your control!"

"I can get you four or five," said Winlaw.

"Five. Make it five. You might lose some of them."

"I'll see what I can do."

"I'm not playing around. Forrest is dead. You need to take this seriously."

"I promise you that I'm taking this seriously, and I'm warning you to watch your tone. Stay where you are. I'll get some reinforcements out there right away."

"Thank you. Tell them to hurry."

Winlaw hung up. Daxton shoved the phone into his left pants pocket, and took Allison's phone out of the right. Password protected. He was no hacker, and he didn't have any great plans for her phone if he could get into it anyway, so he put it back in his pocket.

If she did have a second cell phone, he was screwed. He couldn't just drive away—she'd be able to describe him to the cops. It was possible that she might not want to say a word to anybody, since there was a corpse on her living room floor, but he couldn't count on that. He just needed Winlaw's men to subdue her. He'd hand her over, show his boss what she'd done to Forrest, and try to make the case that she could be an amazing asset for him.

He wasn't going after Allison himself, though. No way in hell.

He hadn't anticipated anything like this. He'd figured that maybe she'd see Forrest coming, fling his spooky ass against the wall, and then while she was doing that Daxton would grab her from behind. The idea that she could just...*crush* him from the inside out like that was terrifying.

Or maybe that's not what she'd done at all. It didn't matter. Other people could worry about that.

He desperately hoped that Winlaw sent the reinforcements out here right away. If they took too long, Daxton might lose what little courage he had left and flee the scene.

DAXTON WAS STILL OUT THERE. Right now Allison really regretted living in such an isolated area. She'd often go hours at a time with no cars driving past her house. If a car did drive past, that could give her the opportunity to run out her back door without him shooting at her.

Or she could get an innocent driver killed.

She walked back into the kitchen and looked into the pots. Tiny bubbles were forming at the bottom, so an intruder bursting into her home now could expect a splash of warm water on his face.

She returned to the living room. A long-shot idea occurred to her. Since her current plan was "wait around to fuck up anybody else who tried to attack her," she decided to give the new idea a try. She opened the door and peeked her head outside, figuring he wouldn't be a skilled enough marksman to get in a head shot from that distance.

"Hey!" she called out.

Daxton looked as if he was unsure whether or not to answer. Finally, he said, "What?"

"Your friend is still alive."

"Is he?"

"Yeah. But he's lost a lot of blood."

"What do you want me to do about it?"

"Call an ambulance."

Daxton shook his head.

"I'm not wearing my contacts so I can't see what you're doing," Allison called out. This wasn't true, but any fake advantage Daxton thought he had might help her at some point.

"I shook my head," Daxton said.

"You don't care if he dies?"

"I assume he's already dead."

"He's not. You could save him."

"The world is a better place with him dead. If I came back inside I'd just spit on the body."

"Why are you still here?" Allison asked.

"You have to sleep sometime."

"So do you."

"That's true."

"Why don't we try to work something out?"

"Nah," said Daxton. "I have nowhere to be right now."

Allison tried again to break his bones. Nothing happened.

"This isn't going to work out for you," she called out. "I very strongly suggest that you leave."

"I'll take that under consideration."

Allison stepped back into her living room and closed the front door. He had to be waiting on reinforcements. She once again thought about taking her chances and fleeing out the back door, but that still didn't seem like a smart idea. For now, she'd just wait.

Ten minutes later, Daxton's phone rang. It was Winlaw.

"They're on the way," he said.

"Yes! Thank you!"

"I'm assuming that you can't possibly be so stupid that you'd make me waste my time."

"I'm not," Daxton assured him. "How long until they get here?"

"Half an hour. They're traveling separately to a meeting spot and then they'll travel to you together. Look for a white van."

"Have the van stop before they see me. Right before the last turn, have them get out and walk. We don't want to give her too much of a heads-up. How many guys? Four or five?"

"Five."

"Fantastic. Thank you!" Daxton didn't know Allison's capabilities, but surely she couldn't take out five guys at once. If they all broke in at the same time, he was confident that at least one of them would survive.

Half an hour. He could keep her inside the house for that long, right?

The pots of water were at a full boil.

Allison's biggest advantage was that, as far as she knew, Daxton didn't want to kill her. Otherwise the dead man on her living room floor could've just shot her in the back. It was entirely possible that the plan had changed now that she'd killed one of them, but the man sneaking up on her with a wet cloth implied that they wanted to kidnap her, not murder her.

Thank God her cell phone had a passcode. They wouldn't be

able to see or respond to Cody's texts. He still had half a day of work left. She could certainly use some help right about now, but she didn't want anybody to get hurt on her behalf, especially Cody.

Every minute or so she'd peek out the window at Daxton. He hadn't left her yard but he was walking up and down the side, never looking away from her house. She wished she could look at him through a different window—if she could see a moment where he was distracted, she could make a sudden run for it. Unfortunately, he'd have to remain distracted while she left her office and hurried to the back door, and that was far too risky.

For the first time in her life, she wished she owned a rifle. It would be wonderful to be able to squeeze off a few shots; scare him away if nothing else.

She still felt awful about what she'd done to his unborn child. But once he had somebody break into her home to kidnap her, he became the bad guy, and she'd worry about her conscience after she'd escaped. For now, he was the enemy, and she was determined to survive.

Allison walked back into the living room. She couldn't believe how large the pool of blood had become. She was tempted to throw a blanket over him, but if Daxton returned with more friends, she wanted them to see what she was capable of.

Perhaps she could smear his blood on her face, like war paint.

Nah.

She swished the butcher knife through the air in front of her, imagining that it sliced deep into Daxton's belly. She imagined his look of anguish as he desperately tried to keep his intestines from spilling out.

"They're here," said Winlaw.

Daxton was ecstatic. It hadn't even been the full half hour. "Can you have them call me?"

"Sure."

Allison didn't like that Daxton was smiling. He gestured wildly as he spoke on the phone, but he still refused to look away from the house for even a moment. He seemed almost deliriously happy, and that couldn't be good for her.

She scooped up Spiral and shut him in her bedroom to keep him safe, just in case.

"Hey," said a low voice over the phone that Daxton didn't immediately recognize.

"All five of you are here, right?" Daxton asked.

"Yep."

"Perfect, perfect. You'll need to move fast. She's keeping an eye on her yard, so you'll basically just rush the house, break the front window, and all five of you go after her at once. Don't do it like some martial arts flick where you go at her one at a time. Five at once. Move fast. Got it?"

"What about you?"

"I'll be watching."

"Not going in?"

Hell no. "I'll be waiting outside in case she escapes."

"You think she can escape all five of us?"

"Maybe. Winlaw told you not to hurt her, right?"

"No. He said not to kill her. He didn't say we couldn't hurt her."

"If she gets banged up that's okay, but don't do anything that might cause traumatic brain injury or anything like that. Like, don't bash her head against a counter."

"No bashing her head against a counter. Got it."

"Be careful," said Daxton. "She's dangerous."

"I think we can handle it."

"Don't get overconfident."

"Is there something you're not telling us?"

It didn't sound like Winlaw had told them they were going after a woman with supernatural abilities. Daxton agreed with that approach; he didn't want them thinking the job was all a big joke, and he also didn't want them to know that at least one of them was probably going to be losing a lot of blood in the next couple of minutes.

"Just knock her out as fast as you can. That's all I'm saying."

"All right. We're on our way."

Daxton hung up. He wanted to point at Allison's house and cackle with laughter. *It's over now, bitch!*

Of course, he didn't know that for sure—she might be able to blink and make all of their heads explode into red mist—but right now he was feeling almost giddy. And simultaneously ready to puke.

The five men came into view. Daxton recognized three of them. Except for his dumbass future son-in-law, Winlaw didn't work with incompetent people, so there was every reason to believe these guys could get the job done. It would've been cool if they were all in matching black suits, but they'd all clearly rushed to the scene wearing whatever they had on when they got the call. It didn't matter. It was a sufficiently intimidating quintet.

"There!" Daxton said, speaking in a loud whisper, gesturing to Allison's home even though it was the only house within sight. "Go! Get her!"

The guy in front, who Daxton didn't know, looked unsure. Without Winlaw's orders, no way would they blindly rush into the house like this. But they *did* have Winlaw's orders, and every instant of hesitation worked in Allison's favor.

"Go!" he repeated.

The five men rushed toward Allison's home.

13

As the five men raced toward her house, Allison hurried into the kitchen. She started to take a deep breath to center herself for the fight ahead, then remembered that she didn't *want* to be calm and centered. She needed raw panic.

She waited.

Her front window shattered.

She picked up the first pot of water.

"Should we split up?" she heard a man ask.

"We were specifically told not to," another answered.

"She's there," said a third. "Behind that closed door."

Allison was not willing to risk her own life to keep them from killing Spiral, but since the plan was for them to find her anyway, it made sense to save her cat and keep them out of the bedroom. She pretended to accidentally bump against the counter.

Seconds later, a man came through the doorway to the

kitchen. He was young and in good shape, wearing a shirt that had obviously been selected for how well it showed off his physique. In a one-on-one fistfight, he'd knock her to the floor with a single punch.

But this was not a fistfight.

She flung the entire pot of boiling water, getting him right in the face.

His shriek was so loud and intense that the other men behind him stopped.

Allison stepped forward, bashing the hot metal against his face. It hissed as it made contact with his flesh. She wrenched it away, taking a large piece of his cheek with it, then struck him again.

He stumbled backwards, clawing at his eyes, and crashed into the men behind him.

Allison grabbed another pot of water.

She threw the water at the group of men. Nobody was unfortunate enough to get hit with the entire pot full this time—it got the closest man more than the others, but the two next to him were also splashed. They all cried out in pain.

Daxton was an idiot. Apparently he'd been so focused on her powers that he didn't consider how threatening she could be in her own kitchen.

She hurled the pot, bashing the closest man in the nose. Blood gushed from his nostrils, mixing with the scalding water, as the pot dropped to the floor.

She grabbed the two remaining pots, one in each hand, and threw them.

The first one was a bad throw that bounced off the doorway. She shouldn't have tried both at once. The second bounced off the man with the broken nose's scalp, spilling its contents all down his face. As he screamed, some uncontrollable instinct made him catch the pot before it fell. It sizzled against his hands and didn't come loose immediately when he tried to drop it.

No time to relax. Allison went for the knives.

IT SOUNDED like things were going badly in there.

Shit.

Five men should've been enough!

Daxton tried to relax. The shrieks of agony didn't mean that all five of the men were going to die. He just needed one of them to do his job. Just one. It would be fine. Perfectly fine.

THE CLOSEST INTRUDER hadn't fallen yet, and Allison didn't want to squander a knife on somebody who was in such terrible shape. Their tactic of all five of them attacking at once would've been more effective if she'd been in the living room or another open space. In the kitchen, the doorway kept them from overwhelming her.

Finally, the closest man, whose burns were so bad that they bled, toppled forward and Allison threw the butcher knife at where his head used to be. It struck the guy right behind him, but hit him handle-first. She threw another knife before the first hit the floor. This one also fell to the floor, though not before the tip hit him in the eye.

Allison kept throwing knives.

The third knife got the man with a bloody eye in the shoulder.

The fourth knife also hit him, but he wouldn't fall.

Unless she wanted to start throwing forks and spoons, she'd have to conserve her utensils. She ran at him and plunged a knife into his throat.

As he fell to the side, she slammed the same knife into the man behind him, stabbing it into his chest several times, hoping she was getting him where the hot water had landed.

The other two men moved out of sight.

Allison stabbed the man a few more times, because though she felt she was doing an admirable job of hanging on to her sanity, she didn't want him to cause future problems simply because she hadn't stabbed him enough times.

The man fell to the floor.

She returned to the counter and traded out the bloody knife for a new one.

None of the three men lying on her kitchen floor appeared to be dead yet, but none of them would last much longer. Soon she'd be in a house with four corpses, tying her record.

Two intruders left. Allison was disappointed that she didn't hear them fleeing out the broken window. She could hear at least one of them breathing—a wonderfully panicked series of breaths—and knew he was still right outside the kitchen door.

He stepped into view, holding a gun.

She ducked beneath the counter as he squeezed off a shot.

OH, no. No, no, no.

That could've been Allison shooting, Daxton supposed, but she'd had plenty of time to retrieve a firearm and he would've heard shots as soon as the men broke into her house. It was much more likely that this was one of Winlaw's men deciding that things were going so terribly that he had to resort to gunfire.

After all of this shit, it couldn't end with Allison dead. Even if he could blame these five idiots, it was still another job that ended in complete disaster. He'd have to run, with or without Maggie.

Daxton took out his gun and climbed through the broken window.

Forrest lay dead on the floor, right where Daxton had left him. Jerry, a short guy who'd cut off some dude's fingers with Daxton a couple of years ago, fired another shot then quickly ducked back out of the doorway. Another man stood behind him. His bearded face was bright red, the skin peeling.

"Don't shoot!" Daxton shouted.

"Fuck you!" Jerry shouted back. He leaned toward the kitchen doorway again.

Daxton shot him in the head.

The bullet struck the side of his skull, right above the ear, and the spray of bone, brains, and blood made it clear that Jerry would not be getting back up as he fell to the floor.

The bearded man ran into the kitchen.

Daxton didn't want to pursue him. Allison was in there. Maybe she already had three corpses piled at her feet, and maybe the other guys still had a chance, but Daxton was getting the hell out of here, gunshots or not.

Allison held up a knife, trying to look as threatening as possible as a bearded man with a scalded face stepped over the first of the soon-to-be-dead men.

She had a pretty good idea of what had happened out there. The guy with the gun had retreated to safety after taking a shot at her, then she heard Daxton tell him not to shoot, and then he took a bullet to the head. So Daxton *really* didn't want her dead, if he was willing to murder his own partners to keep them from killing her.

That was a point in her favor, but the bearded guy was looking pretty homicidal.

"Don't come any closer," she told him, waving the knife.

He came closer.

Allison threw the knife at him.

He moved out of the way.

She picked up another knife.

He reached under his shirt and pulled out a revolver.

"You're not supposed to shoot me," she said.

"You think I give a shit about that?"

"I bet the dead guy behind you wishes he'd given a shit about it."

As they spoke, she tried to make him bleed. But it wasn't working. When she'd killed the first intruder, it was as if her subconscious mind had taken over. Trying to make a man bleed from his ears, nose, and eyes on purpose was having no effect.

But he hadn't shot her yet.

"Put the knife down," he said.

"No."

"Put it down or I'll shoot you in the throat."

"Shoot me and you'll be punished."

The man laughed and scratched at his face, peeling off a piece of skin. "With the body count you've racked up, you think I care about getting in trouble? I'll take pictures of the bodies all over your floor. I'm pretty sure my boss will understand. Put the knife down."

If this turned into a duel, the lady with the knife had no chance against the man with the gun. And though he hadn't fired, she was pretty sure he would if she didn't comply. So she placed the knife down on the counter.

"Now what?" she asked.

"Now you're going to walk outside with me, nice and calm. There's no reason anybody else has to get hurt."

That didn't sound like a good outcome. If Allison wanted to leave with the man, she could've just let the first guy press his wet rag into her face and saved herself the cost of a new carpet.

She had to make her ability work.

She had to summon all of the fury and terror that she was feeling right now.

Lose control. Go completely feral.

Allison squeezed her eyes shut, threw back her head, and screamed as loud as she could.

She shrieked until she had no breath left.

Before she opened her eyes, she heard a thump. It sounded very much like a gun falling onto the tile floor.

When she opened them, the bearded man was still standing. His beard was drenched with the blood that was gushing from his mouth. His left eye dangled from its socket. His right eye was still in its proper location, but bugged out like a cartoon character.

He said something she couldn't understand. It sounded like a plea for help.

"Just fucking fall," she told him.

The man started to drop to the floor, but braced himself against the counter in time.

Allison picked up the knife and stabbed him in the face.

He fell.

At some point very soon Allison was going to have to have a nervous breakdown over what had just happened, complete with twitching in the fetal position, but for now she was going to focus on her survival.

She went around the counter, then bent down and picked up the man's gun. The handle was slick with blood.

She glanced at the other bodies on the floor. None of them looked even remotely threatening to her anymore, but she'd watched her share of slasher flicks where the heroine failed to ensure that the killer was sufficiently dead and paid the price.

After pulling the knife out of the bearded man's face, she stabbed the fallen men in the throats, three times each. They would not be getting back up.

She left the knife buried in the last man's throat, then walked into the living room with the gun. Daxton wasn't there.

She caught a glimpse of him outside, running away from the house.

Allison climbed out the window and went after him.

14

Daxton nearly shit his pants as the gunshot rang out and he realized that Allison was shooting at him. Five reinforcements had broken into her home, and now he was fleeing for his life. This was insane.

He didn't like his chances of not getting shot before he reached his car.

He took out his gun—a challenge while running—then spun around.

Allison, who was standing right outside her house, shot at him again. They were about two hundred feet apart, and he couldn't tell how close she came to hitting him.

He couldn't just let her shoot him. Maybe he could hit her in the leg.

He took quick aim and fired.

The shot shattered some glass in the already broken living room window. She fired back, and though Daxton couldn't quite feel the swish of wind as the bullet sailed past his head, she'd come unnervingly close to hitting him.

She let out a shriek.

Daxton's knees buckled and he immediately got a headache as bad as his occasional migraines. He dropped the gun. He stumbled forward a couple of steps, dizzy.

No. He couldn't meet Forrest's fate. He had to flee.

He forced himself to turn around and run. He almost collapsed but maintained his footing and hurried toward the edge of her yard. Allison continued screaming, but he wasn't bleeding and none of his teeth had fallen out. His headache quickly began to fade as he made it toward the road and ran for his car.

She stopped screaming and resumed shooting.

Two shots, one right after another. Neither of them hit him.

Daxton didn't care how angry Winlaw was after this. He just needed to get away from her.

He made it to his car. Got into the driver's seat. Fumbled to get his keys out of his pocket.

A shot fired through the rear windshield, sailed past his head, and put a hole in the front windshield.

Daxton yelped in surprise and ducked down.

More shots. The car sunk down a bit. She was shooting his fucking tires!

Daxton opened the car door again and got out, keeping himself low. He bobbed his head up and peeked through the window just long enough to see Allison walking toward him with the gun extended. That bitch was moving with *purpose.*

She kept walking as she let out another shriek.

DAXTON TOOK OFF RUNNING. This scream seemed to have had no impact on him.

It was probably because she was chasing after the chickenshit and shooting up his car, so she wasn't as scared or panicked as she needed to be for her powers to work.

She'd simply have to keep using the gun.

As he ran down the road, she took another shot at him.

Missed.

Dammit. This was her first time firing a gun, and she was obviously terrible at it, though it would help if she didn't have a moving target.

She didn't know how many bullets were in the gun. It wasn't a six-shooter—she'd already shot more than that. She might be out of ammunition. Best to try to run him down and save her next shot for when she was much closer.

If only she was in better shape. She did a lot of walking. Not much sprinting. If she was pursuing him during a vigorous hike through the woods, he'd be a goner, but in a race like this, he was pulling ahead.

Did it matter if he got away?

Yeah, it did. She didn't want him coming back with even more men. This time they'd know that "break her front window and charge into the kitchen" was a poor tactical approach. She had to hunt Daxton down and make this problem go away.

DAXTON RAN past the van that had brought the other morons

here. He didn't have the keys, so there was no reason to try to get inside.

Five men should've been able to catch her. This wasn't on him. He'd warned Winlaw that Allison was dangerous. He should've sent better men, or more men. He should have listened. This wasn't his fault. Not his fault.

He veered off the road into the woods.

It was uneven terrain but he didn't dare to slow down. If he took a fall...well, he was dead. He'd just have to hope not to take a fall.

The worst part was that she'd offered to pay the fucking medical bills. If he'd come back alone to continue the scam, instead of bringing that psychopath Forrest along, he'd be on his way home with a check right now.

He tripped. Lurched forward. Bashed into a tree.

Shook it off and kept going.

When Daxton ran into the woods, Allison decided not to pursue him.

There was too much opportunity for something to go wrong. She could trip. He could hide and surprise her. She could lose him completely and then waste time running around the woods that could be spent grabbing her bug out bag from home and getting the hell out of town.

And though she didn't have any close neighbors, it wasn't as if there were no homes for miles around. Somebody could've heard the gunfire and called the police. If the cops showed up, running through the woods with a gun like a crazy woman wouldn't be a good look for her.

She returned to her home.

She climbed in through the broken front window. The dark pool around the first dead man didn't seem to have expanded since she left, so maybe he'd finally bled out. The man Daxton had shot in the head was still bleeding.

She looked into the kitchen. All three men in there were motionless and presumably dead.

Allison turned away and vomited.

Everything hit her at once. She'd murdered all of these men! In self-defense, yes, but she'd stabbed a man in the face! She'd chased after Daxton with every intention of killing him!

Survival instinct or not, she was a monster.

What was she supposed to do? She couldn't call Cody over here to help her get rid of a half-dozen corpses. He wouldn't agree to help her, and even if he did, somebody who would help a woman he'd just met dispose of a bunch of dead bodies was not a good person to have in your life.

Allison staggered away from the mess and collapsed onto the couch. She sat there for a few moments, trying to catch her breath, trying not to start sobbing and convulsing and having a complete mental breakdown.

Hopefully she could stop the mental breakdown, but she couldn't stop the sobbing and convulsing. Though she needed to get out of there, she couldn't force herself off the couch.

Maybe she should call the police.

She was allowed to defend herself from home intruders, right?

I don't know what happened to that guy, she could say, as investigators questioned the fact that all of his teeth had fallen out. What were they going to do, accuse her of killing him with her mind?

If she took credit for the boiling water and the knives, and claimed to have, say, bashed the toothless guy in the face with a pot, would it make a difference if forensics concluded that not everything matched up? *"I knocked out his teeth with a metal pot." "Is that so? Our examination shows that his teeth fell out on their own." "Fine. His teeth coincidentally just happened to fall out right before I hit him with the pot. Are you happy?"*

How would she explain the guy whose eyeball was dangling from its stalk?

Did it matter?

If she said that the men broke into her house and she killed all of them, was it a problem if there were unexplained elements? Maybe she hit him so hard with the pot that his eye popped out. Professional examiners were not going to conclude that there were supernatural powers at work. If she wasn't lying about killing them, and if she told the truth about everything except for the unexplainable stuff, would she be in trouble?

She'd killed people before and the police let her go.

Of course, she'd been ten years old.

She definitely didn't want the celebrity that would come from violently slaughtering six men. There'd be reporters everywhere. She'd be frantic. Bad things could happen.

Bad things could happen if the police interrogated her.

Fuck! Calling the cops *seemed* like the right choice, but if a detective started gushing blood from his eyes while on camera asking her questions, who knew what might happen to her? She couldn't be around people during stressful situations. That was the whole goddamn problem in her life.

What was she going to say? *"Hey, there are mangled bodies all over my house, but please don't take me out of my happy place when you ask about them. Nothing but softball questions, please."*

How could she report this to the authorities without putting innocent people at risk?

DAXTON TWISTED HIS ANKLE, pitched forward, and slammed into the ground.

As he lay there, utterly miserable, he didn't hear any footsteps.

He'd been running for a few minutes, and there was no evidence that Allison was still following him. Maybe she'd given up. Maybe he was safe.

"Safe," of course, was a relative term now.

The last thing in the world he wanted to do right now was report the incident to Winlaw, but the sooner he did, the more likely it was that his boss would absolve him from responsibility. He stood up and started walking, not bothering to brush the dirt and leaves off his clothes. He took out his phone and made the call.

"Is it done?" asked Winlaw.

"They're all dead," said Daxton. "Every one of them."

"I beg your pardon?"

"All five of them are dead. Forrest is dead. Everybody's fucking dead."

"What are you trying to pull here, Daxton?"

"I'm being completely honest with you. Call them. None of them will answer. They're all dead. You want to come out here and see for yourself?"

"Where are you now?"

"I'm in the woods. I barely got away. Look, sir, I tried to do something great for you, but you didn't send enough men. I asked for a dozen. A dozen men could've caught her. This isn't my fault."

"I don't have a dozen men at my immediate disposal."

"Well, that's not on me. If you don't have the resources to get the job done it's not my fault. You can't blame me for this."

"I'm sorry, Daxton, but you don't get to decide where I place my blame. The way I see it, you're worthless to me. At this point I might as well cut my losses and watch you and your girlfriend die ghastly deaths. Our business relationship is now over."

"No, please, sir, let's—"

"Discuss it? Okay. Turn yourself in. Right now. Be here in thirty minutes, accept the fate that's in store for you, and I'll let Maggie live. Sacrifice yourself for your unborn child. Otherwise, I'll catch you, and I'll be in an even worse mood when I inflict the suffering. Goodbye."

"No! No! Mr. Winlaw—" Too late. He'd already hung up.

Spiral!

Allison got up off the couch and hurried over to her bedroom door. As far as she knew her abilities didn't work on animals, but she'd never tried the "shriek" approach before.

She opened the door. Spiral lay on the bed.

He looked asleep.

She petted his head and he looked up, annoyed to have been awakened. He was okay.

She left him on the bed and returned to the living room.

Something was buzzing.

A cell phone.

It was in the pocket of the man who Daxton had shot. She slid it out and looked at the display, which said "Boss Man." She accepted the call but said nothing.

"Hello?" asked a man on the other end.

"Who is this?" she asked.

"Who is *this*?"

Allison said nothing.

"Is this Allison?"

She hesitated. "Yes."

"Is it true that you killed six of my employees?"

"Yes," she said. "I completely fucked them up. They're all dead on my floor. Do you want pictures? I'll send pictures." Without waiting for him to answer, she switched to the camera and took quick photographs of each of the dead men. She texted them to Boss Man. "Do you believe me, asshole?"

"I do."

"That'll happen to you and anybody else you send after me. Do you understand? Leave me the fuck alone, whoever you are."

The man on the other end chuckled. "Noted. So, Allison, let's talk."

15

Maggie didn't answer her phone. Daxton texted her to call him back immediately, then called again. She practically had that cell phone surgically grafted to her right hand, but *now* she wasn't going to answer?

She answered. "Hi."

"Why didn't you pick up the first time?"

"I'm on the toilet. I thought it could wait."

"It can't. Get out of the apartment. Go somewhere. It doesn't matter where. Not with your family—not anyplace anybody would think to look."

"What did you do to us?" Maggie asked.

"Mr. Winlaw is coming after you. Grab your purse and get the hell out of there. Just get in the car and drive. Don't tell me where you're going. Answer the phone if I call but don't call me. Okay?"

"Seriously, Daxton, what did you do?"

"I didn't do shit! This isn't on me! That bitch is a raging psychopath, and she killed six of Winlaw's men."

"Wait, what?"

"I barely got out alive. She might still be trying to hunt me down. Winlaw is having a meltdown over it and he's coming after you, so I need you to shut the fuck up and do what I say, all right? Get out of town. Get in the car and just drive. Don't use credit cards for anything. All right?"

"Okay."

"I'll call you as soon as I can."

"Where are you now?"

"I'm walking around in some woods. Go. Take this seriously. I love you."

Maggie hung up.

She'd do what he said. Daxton was sure of it.

He was deeply in love with her and would do almost anything for his child, but he wasn't going to sacrifice himself for them. A quick death? Maybe. But not the hell on earth that Winlaw had planned for him. Not a chance. So if she was too stupid to get out of town like he told her to...well, he'd be devastated, but he wasn't going to march into Winlaw's office and give himself up.

Maybe there was still an opportunity for redemption. It was certainly better to die at Allison's hands than Winlaw's—at least hers would be quick. Numbers and brute force didn't work. He'd have to take her by surprise.

He wanted to get as far away from here as possible, but that meant a life of constant fear, for as long as it took him to get caught. Which might not be very long. If he still somehow managed to subdue Allison and deliver her, Winlaw might forgive him. Perhaps let him off the hook after another savage beating. After all, Allison was even more dangerous—and therefore more useful—than Daxton had ever imagined.

Dammit! That's how he should have pitched it when he called Winlaw! Instead of treating the massacre as a disaster, he should have reported it as a *positive* development. *"The bad news is, everybody you sent over here is dead. The good news is, with Allison under your control, you could rule this city!"* It sounded like cheesy supervillain shit...but it was basically the truth, right? If Allison could kill people with her mind, and Winlaw could control Allison, he'd be unstoppable.

But Daxton couldn't call him now. *"Hey, boss, I thought of a much better way to phrase the news."* He'd totally screwed up. Again.

He wandered through the woods for a few minutes, unsure which way to go. If he got lost in these frickin' woods, he deserved to die. His phone had a GPS, but he might not be able to return to his apartment, and he should conserve battery power for now. It wasn't like he was in the middle of some gigantic forest—it was the woods next to Allison's house. What kind of idiot could lose his way out here, in daylight?

He only bumbled around for a couple more minutes before seeing the road. He emerged from the woods, trying to work out a plan. She wouldn't expect him to come right back. That could work in his favor.

What other advantage could he gain?

He heard a car approaching, so he stepped back into the woods, out of sight.

The car drove past.

Daxton didn't believe in God or any other higher power, but

damn, *somebody* was looking out for him. He'd just been given an amazing opportunity, and he wasn't going to waste it.

"WHY WOULD I want to talk to you?" Allison asked.

"Because I can make your life much easier, or I can make it much more difficult," said the man on the other end. "For now, let's pretend that I'm going to make it easier. One of my employees told me that you have a certain gift. Is there any truth to that?"

"What kind of gift?"

"You tell me."

"I don't even know who you are."

"My name is Dominick Winlaw. I'm not mad at you. I'm fascinated. How did you kill those men?"

"I drenched them with boiling water then stabbed the shit out of them."

"I heard otherwise."

"What did you hear?"

"You want me to be blunt? Fine, I'll be blunt. I heard that you have telekinetic powers."

"And you believed that?"

"No," said Winlaw. "I thought it was ridiculous. Then you sent me pictures of six dead bodies on your floor and it suddenly didn't seem as far-fetched."

"That's fair. But I personally would go through a lot more possibilities before I settled on magic."

"You're absolutely right. And at this point I don't even care. Regardless of how you did it, the fact is that you killed several of my men. I'm not saying that these were world class assassins, but still, it's a pretty impressive feat."

"They were stupid."

"How so?"

"I'm not telling," said Allison. "If you send more people after me, I want them to make the same stupid mistakes."

Winlaw laughed. "I like you."

"I'm hanging up now, because I feel like you're trying to distract me."

"Hear me out. I'll be brief. If you've already called the police and they're on their way, we have nothing more to say to each other. Is that the case?"

Allison wasn't sure if she should tell the truth or not. "Maybe."

"For now, I'll take that as a no. I'll be perfectly honest with you. Given the choice, I would rather *not* have the police show up and find those dead men in your house. It's just the way I feel. If you haven't called the police yet, then maybe you feel the same way. If we both feel the same way, then suddenly I could become very useful to you."

Allison looked at all of the gore in her kitchen. Her life would be much easier if she didn't have to explain it to the authorities. Still, since these mutilated bodies were Winlaw's employees, she couldn't exactly trust him. "I'm listening."

"I'll send out a cleanup crew. They'll make the bodies disappear. You'll come home to a corpse-free home and a nice new carpet. They work quickly. It will be like this never happened."

If only...

"Then what?" Allison asked.

"Then hopefully you'll be willing to have another conversation with me. It's your choice. I'll be satisfied just to make the bodies go away. That's a pretty good win-win first step, don't you think? Again, if you've called the police, then this whole discussion is moot, but you haven't hung up on me yet."

Though not everything Allison did in her life was a master class in exquisite decision-making, she also wasn't a complete idiot. Winlaw wouldn't clean up her mess with no strings attached. He'd leave somebody behind, perhaps hiding in her closet. Or he'd install hidden cameras, or an explosive device to blow her up when she opened the refrigerator. He'd do *something*, and she'd have to be absurdly gullible to trust him.

Unless she had no plans to return.

Let him clean up the bodies while she and Spiral got the hell out of town forever. There would be some logistical issues, like selling the house, that would be a pain in the ass, but she'd take that over trying to dispose of a bunch of mangled corpses.

"All right," she said. "You can clean up my place. I won't need to leave a key—your guys can come in through the broken window."

"Thank you," said Winlaw. "I hope this is the beginning of a beautiful partnership."

She wondered if he was trying to kind-of quote *Casablanca*. Then she felt a little better knowing that if she could wonder something as trivial as that, she wasn't having a complete nervous breakdown.

Allison hung up. She didn't know how long she had before the cleaning crew got here. Probably not very long. She hurried into her office and grabbed her work laptop, then got her bug out bag from her bedroom closet. It was an oversized duffel bag filled with cash, essential documents, and other items she'd need for her time on the road.

She quickly took that stuff out to her car and put it in the trunk, then went back inside to collect Spiral. The cat was startled by her aggressive attempt to scoop him up and tried to get away, but one nice thing about an old cat was that they were easy to catch. The bug out bag already had a small amount of cat food and litter, saving her thirty potentially crucial seconds.

Time to go.

No, wait. She was a mess. Even if it cost her a couple of extra minutes, she had to change out of her bloody clothes and rinse off.

She took a very fast shower, then got dressed in jeans and a dark blue sweatshirt. If she missed a spot, she didn't want any blood visibly soaking through.

Then she got in her car and sped off, with no destination in mind except to get as far away from here as possible.

16

Since Allison wasn't answering any of his text messages or phone calls, Cody took a half-day at work to go check on her. She might be angry with him, but she was clearly in a very bad place, and without her assurance that she was okay he needed to make sure she wasn't lying in a bathtub filled with bloody water.

He had no idea if a relationship between the two of them could work out, but he liked the idea of being the *less* messed-up of the two. Usually he was the weird one. The whole "*Hey, I may freak out and break your arm in my sleep*," was less of an issue with somebody who could break bones with her mind.

Did he believe her?

Pretty much, yeah.

He'd seen—with one hundred percent certainty—Allison stop the pregnant woman from falling without actually touching her.

Some might say that if a woman had the power to severely

harm or kill you with her mind, and she couldn't control this power, it was best not to date her. There was a definite logic to that point of view. Cody couldn't help his infatuation, though, and while she didn't necessarily *need* him in her life, surely the fact that he hadn't run screaming from her meant that she might *want* him to stick around. He'd be good for her. Give her an extra little smidgen of happiness.

They'd have to be careful, but Cody was a pretty observant guy. If Allison's emotions were rising, he'd politely but quickly excuse himself. He'd learn to spot the signs. They could figure this out.

Assuming she hadn't done something terrible.

He'd stay optimistic. Ignoring his messages and calls didn't mean she was suicidal. Hell, for all he knew, she could've accidentally dropped her phone into the toilet and it was sitting in a bowl of rice right now, even though the rice trick didn't actually work.

He'd find out soon. He was almost to her house.

In his rearview mirror, Cody saw a man step out of the woods behind him. The man began to frantically wave his hands over his head, trying to get his attention. Cody stopped the car and the man hurried toward it.

This seemed like something that Cody probably should not get involved with, but the man wasn't carrying a roaring chainsaw, so Cody would at least find out what he wanted. He hoped it had nothing to do with Allison, though a guy coming out of the woods and flagging him down very close to Allison's home seemed pretty unlikely to be a complete coincidence.

The man opened the door and got into the passenger seat. As he slammed the door closed, Cody recognized him. It was the husband or boyfriend of the pregnant woman. Cody suddenly very much wished he'd just kept driving.

Before Cody could say anything, the man took out a gun and shoved it against Cody's side.

"Hey, asshole, you're my prisoner now." The man was twitchy, almost like a drug addict having withdrawals. "If I get the slightest hint that you're going to try something, I'll pull the trigger. The bullet goes in one side, out the other, and you die a slow agonizing death. Got it?"

Cody nodded. He'd never even held a gun, much less been threatened with one. He wasn't going to succumb to panic, though. He'd do whatever it took to stay calm. He'd get through this.

"What are you doing here?" the man asked.

Cody couldn't think of a credible lie, at least not with a gun pressed against his side. "Checking on Allison."

"Why?"

"She might be in trouble. I mean, obviously she's in trouble. What did you do to her?"

"I didn't do shit to her."

"So she's okay?"

"As far as I know. Who the hell are you? I saw you on the street when my girlfriend fell. How do you know Allison?"

"We became friends after that. She was really upset and I talked to her to calm her down. She stopped responding to my texts so I drove out here to make sure nothing was wrong." Cody tried to give the man a friendly smile. "I'm Cody."

"I'm Daxton. I guess we're best buddies now, huh?"

"I guess."

"Cody, you are the bright spot in what has been an

amazingly shitty day. You're going to help me out. What you're *not* going to do is get an inflated sense of your self-worth. I will shoot you without a moment of hesitation. You are completely expendable to me. Are we clear?"

"Yeah, we're clear."

"Does Allison trust you?"

"I guess."

"That's not good enough."

"I only met her yesterday."

"And yet you drove out here to check on her."

"Right," said Cody. "But that has nothing to do with whether or not she trusts me. Maybe I'm a lunatic stalker."

"Are you trying to be funny?"

"I don't know what I was trying to be."

"Don't try to amuse me," said Daxton. "I'm not in the mood. Drive to her house."

"Okay." Cody resumed driving. He needed to come up with some sort of plan, but he had no reason to doubt that Daxton would indeed shoot him. The loss of his unborn child had driven the man murderously insane. What kind of ingenious plan could Cody concoct with the barrel of a gun pressed against him? His only current option seemed to be: *do what the scary man says*. He didn't want anything bad to happen to Allison, but he didn't want to get shot in the gut for her.

He drove past a van and an empty car parked on the side of the street. Daxton's? It didn't matter. No reason to ask.

Around the corner, he saw Allison's home, a small place with a huge yard.

"Fuck," said Daxton.

"What?"

"Her car's gone."

"I didn't see her drive by."

"Well, no shit. She must have gone the other way."

"What do you want me to do?" Cody asked.

"Park in her driveway."

Cody drove up right in front of Allison's home. The front window was shattered, which seemed like a very bad sign.

"Now what?"

"Any chance you know the passcode for her phone?"

"Do you have her phone?"

"Are you seriously going to ask me a dumb question like that?" asked Daxton.

"No, I don't know her passcode. Why would I?"

"I don't know. I didn't think you did, but maybe you watched her unlock it after you two were done fucking last night."

Cody didn't respond to that.

"Get out of the car," Daxton told him. "We're going inside."

They both got out. Cody didn't even consider making a run for it—no way would he make it to the safety of the woods before Daxton squeezed off a few shots.

Daxton waved the gun at him. "Let's go." They walked over to the house. "Try the front door."

Cody turned the doorknob. "It's locked."

"We're going through the window, then. Are you squeamish?"

"Yes."

"It's horrific in there. Your girlfriend left a pile of corpses behind. You can throw up if you can't keep your lunch down, or you can cry, or curse God, or whatever you need to do as long as you don't make any sudden movements. I'll be more than happy to add another body to the pile."

"Allison killed people?" Cody asked. His mouth had suddenly gone dry.

"That's what I just said. You think I'd make something like that up? Climb on in."

Cody walked over to the front window and peered inside. There was indeed a dead body on the floor—no, two of them. And lots of blood.

He looked back at Daxton. "Who are they?"

"My co-workers."

"Why did she kill them?"

"It's not Q&A time. Get in there."

Cody climbed through the window and into Allison's living room. He slapped his hand over his mouth and tried to keep from vomiting, even though Daxton had given him permission to do so. He was able to choke it down while Daxton climbed into the living room after him.

"Feeling okay?" Daxton asked.

Cody nodded.

Daxton pointed to the dead man in the center of the room. "Know what your girlfriend did to him? Looked at him. That's all she did. His teeth fell out and he started bleeding from all over. I bet if we took off his clothes we'd see that he was bleeding from *all* over, but we're not gonna do that."

"What are we doing in here?"

"We're making sure she's not hiding."

"You said her car was gone."

"Could be a fake-out."

"You think she moved the car, then went back and hid in the house?"

"No," said Daxton. "I don't think she did that, but I'm checking to rule out that possibility. The reason my life has turned to shit is that I didn't make sure an apartment was properly searched. The kitchen will probably be worse, so you might as well get it over with and take a look."

"That's okay, I believe you," said Cody.

"I wasn't presenting an option."

Cody walked across a blood-free path on the carpet and looked into the kitchen. It was indeed worse. Twice as many dead bodies in there. Cody managed to once again keep down the vomit, but it was a narrower victory this time. He turned away quickly, hoping Daxton wouldn't consider that a sudden movement.

"Nasty, huh?" Daxton asked.

Those weren't men that she killed by breaking their bones with her mind. There were stab wounds. Burns. Either Allison's powers had more facets than she'd told him about, or she'd fought back through non-supernatural means.

"If she can do that, do you even want to find her?" Cody asked.

"Well, Cody, that's an interesting question. If it were up to me, I'd douse this place in gasoline, set it on fire, and never think of it or her again. Unfortunately, I pretty much have to catch her if I ever want another moment of peace in my life." For a second Daxton looked like he might burst into tears.

"So your girlfriend made you do this?"

Daxton looked confused. "What?"

The chain of events had seemed pretty obvious. Allison

causes girlfriend to lose baby. Boyfriend loses grip on sanity and vows revenge. Boyfriend brings people over to help him get this revenge. Bloodbath ensues.

So why did Daxton seem surprised by Cody asking if his girlfriend made him do this? He said it wasn't up to him. Who else would it be up to? This was revenge for the dead baby, right?

Cody didn't clarify his question. He just looked at Daxton.

Daxton broke eye contact and then seemed to understand the question. "Yeah," he said. "She wants me to make things right."

He was lying. Something else was going on here. These men didn't break into Allison's home to get revenge for the accident. Maybe Daxton was evil, not just distraught.

As Cody glanced around at the carnage, he suddenly came up with a plan that could actually work. "Listen," he said. "I barely know her. Hell, you've known her a few seconds longer than I have. We didn't sleep together. I came here wanting to help her, but I didn't know she was capable of this." He gestured to the dead bodies. "I thought she was kind of weird. I didn't know she was a killing machine."

Daxton chuckled. "Killing machine. Melodramatic but accurate."

"I'm not on her side anymore. I'm not saying I'm on your side, since you keep threatening to shoot me, but you can't seriously believe that I'm going to protect somebody who would slaughter people like this, can you? We need to stop her before she does this to anybody else. Before she kills another baby. She killed your baby, right?"

"Yes."

Maybe Daxton was a skilled liar in other circumstances, but

he was a terrible liar when he was losing his mind. Allison didn't kill his baby. He'd made that up. Why? What kind of sicko would do such a thing?

It didn't matter right now.

"Then let's get her," said Cody.

"How?"

"I don't know. What was your plan?"

"To search the place."

"Let's search the place."

Cody hoped that Daxton would lower the gun, but he kept it pointed at him as they went from room to room. Upon Daxton's instructions, Cody looked under her bed, in her closet, and anywhere else she might be hiding. She wasn't there, unless her powers included invisibility. The idea that she'd moved her car and then returned to the house had been a real stretch anyway.

"What now?" Cody asked.

"Where do you think she might have gone?"

"I have no idea."

"Your place, maybe?"

"Maybe." Cody didn't believe that Allison would show up at his place seeking help. That would put him in danger, and she didn't seem like the kind of person who would drag him into this mess. But he didn't want Daxton to think he was out of options, and that he might as well cut his losses, shoot Cody in the back of the head, and run. "We can check. She obviously doesn't have a key or anything, but if she's truly in trouble she might hang out there and wait."

Daxton nodded. "She might."

"It's a long shot. I won't lie to you."

"Can't hurt to check. Are you in a house or an apartment?"

"Apartment."

"So there'd be security cameras. I guess it *can* hurt to check."

"I'm not sure if there are security cameras," said Cody. "I've never really noticed any."

"What we need to do is find somebody who can get into her phone. You're pretty nerdy—do you have any friends who can crack a passcode?"

Cody didn't. For a split second he considered lying about this, to buy himself some more time, but when that time ran out he'd probably get shot. "No, sorry."

Daxton slapped himself in the forehead, so hard that it made Cody flinch. This guy was having definite problems.

"I can drive you wherever you want to go," said Cody. "My place, your place, wherever."

"You just want to get away from all of these corpses."

"Well, yeah, that's part of it."

Daxton turned toward the window. A light blue van with soap bubbles painted on the side—the logo for a non-existent carpet cleaning service—pulled into the driveway, parking right behind Cody's vehicle.

"Is that her?" Cody asked.

Daxton shook his head. "No. Fuck. *Fuck.*"

"Who is it?"

"Cleaning crew."

17

Daxton considered fleeing out the back door with Cody, but the guys on the cleanup crew were likely to recognize his car, so they'd know he was still in the area. He didn't relish the thought of wandering through the woods with a hostage. Too many ways that could go wrong.

He'd just have to smile and hope for the best.

"Do we run?" Cody asked.

"Nope. You don't say a word unless I ask you a direct question. They're here to get rid of the dead bodies, so if I was going to kill you, the best possible time would be while they're right here to haul you away. Saves me some trouble. With that in mind, I'm going to very strongly encourage you to be on your best possible behavior."

"I won't say a word unless you ask me a direct question," said Cody.

"Good boy."

Two men got out of the van. Daxton recognized both of

them: Vincent Long and Matt Borland, Mr. Winlaw's standard hires for this type of work. Daxton wasn't drinking buddies with them but they were on friendly enough terms.

He walked right up to the broken window. "Hey!" he called out. "It's Daxton! Just letting you know I'm in here!"

Vincent and Matt exchanged a glance then walked toward the house. Daxton unlocked the front door then pulled Cody into the center of the room, right at the edge of Forrest's pool of blood.

The door opened and the cleanup crew stepped inside. Vincent and Matt looked like father and son, though they weren't related. Vincent was in his thirties, handsome, and energetic, while Matt looked like Vincent after twenty years of being beaten down by life. They were both dressed like sanitation workers and wore rubber gloves.

"Hi, guys," said Daxton. He decided not to smile. He didn't want them to think he was trying too hard to pretend that everything was all right.

"Who's that?" Matt asked.

"He's my asset. He can lead me to the girl."

"You know, Winlaw is having a complete fit," said Vincent. "You're supposed to be on your way over there."

"Yeah, yeah, I was going to. Had car problems. She shot my tires out. I was going to make Cody drive me over there."

"No, you weren't," said Matt. "Not unless you're a suicidal idiot. If I were you, I'd be on my way to the Mexican border right now. Or the Canadian one. One of the borders."

Vincent walked past them and looked into the kitchen. "Damn, Daxton. This is way worse than the last mess of yours we had to clean up."

"Neither of them were my fault."

"Look at these guys. Look at this one's eyeball. One chick really did all of this?"

Daxton pointed to the man he'd shot in the head. "I did that one. He was trying to kill her, when Mr. Winlaw specifically demanded that she be captured. She did the other five."

"She's vicious. Matt, you should take a look. Their skin is all red and bubbly and stuff. These are some seriously fucked up gentlemen on this kitchen floor."

"I'll see them when we put them in the bags," said Matt.

"It's gnarly. Nowhere near as bad as Daxton will look if he's dumb enough to turn himself in, but gnarly."

"You should see Forrest's mouth," said Daxton.

Vincent walked over to Forrest, crouched down, and rolled him over. He opened Forrest's mouth with a pair of gloved fingers. "Oh, damn, where'd his teeth go?"

"She knocked them out."

"High kick?"

"Something like that."

"Wow. That's crazy." Vincent stood back up. "Oh, yeah, I see them on the floor. Does the Tooth Fairy pay you for other people's teeth, or do they have to be your own?"

"I don't know the loopholes," said Daxton.

"Do you know how much kids get for teeth these days?" asked Matt. "I've heard of kids getting five bucks. I got a quarter. I'd knock out my permanent teeth for five bucks a pop."

"Anyway," said Daxton, "I'll leave you guys to it."

"Yeah, you'd better be on your way," said Vincent. "Don't worry. We won't tell Winlaw we saw you."

"Thank you."

"You want us to get rid of your car?"

Daxton considered that. He still hoped to reconcile with Winlaw somehow, in which case he'd regret ditching his car. And if he did have to murder Cody and get out of town, he didn't want to be driving a missing man's vehicle. "No, that's okay. If you could get it off the side of the road and tow it to the driveway, I'd really appreciate it."

"Not a problem. We have to get rid of the other van anyway."

"You guys are awesome."

"Hey, we're all in this together," said Vincent. "Oh, and leave him with us."

Daxton frowned. "Excuse me?"

"Was I unclear? Sorry about that. Sometimes I forget to enunciate. Leave the asset with us."

"Why would I do that?"

"You said he could lead you to the girl," said Vincent. "That makes him valuable to Winlaw, which makes him valuable to us. We're doing you a huge favor by not ratting you out right now, so you're going to do us a favor in return."

Daxton shook his head. "No. No way. He's my only bargaining chip. You take him away and I'm dead for sure."

"Not just dead," said Vincent. "Kirkwooded. Is there a past tense form of that? There'd have to be, right? Winlaw will Kirkwood you, after which you'll be Kirkwooded." He glanced over at Matt. "That's correct, right?"

"Sounds correct to me."

"C'mon, guys. You can't do this to me. You're leaving me with nothing."

"I disagree," said Matt. "We're leaving you with a car and a head start. You get on the road now and floor that gas pedal, you may just be okay."

"Please don't do this," said Daxton. "I'll beg. I'll get down on my knees and beg. I don't care—I've got no pride left. He's going after Maggie."

"Don't worry," said Vincent. "Winlaw wouldn't hurt a pregnant woman."

He and Matt looked at each other, then burst into laughter, because of course Winlaw would.

"I'm begging you," said Daxton.

"You already said that," Vincent told him. "Make you a deal. Get down on your knees right there in all of Forrest's blood and muck, kneel right on a few of his teeth, and beg us with all of your heart, and maybe we'll reconsider."

"Fuck you," said Daxton. He'd humiliate himself without hesitation if he thought they'd really let him leave with Cody. But they wouldn't. They'd point and laugh, and Daxton would walk out of the house with bloody knees and no hostage.

Cody looked positively terrified. As well he should.

"He keeps trying to escape," said Daxton. "Good luck finishing the job while babysitting him."

"We appreciate your concern," said Matt.

"Winlaw's going to kill him." Daxton figured he might as well let Cody know that he was basically doomed. He'd rather Cody die in an escape attempt than let these assholes get the credit for delivering him.

"Well, duh," said Vincent.

"You don't think I can shoot both of you?" Daxton asked.

"No," said Matt. "We don't."

Daxton pointed his gun at Cody's head. "Maybe I'll kill him myself."

"That would just piss us off," said Vincent. "I think you should be thankful we're not dragging *you* in to see Winlaw—which would earn us points with the big guy, believe me. Take my advice and drive away from here."

Daxton lowered the gun. He had no other play.

"Give me the keys," he told Cody.

"I'm not valuable at all," Cody said to Vincent and Matt. "Like I was telling him, I barely know Allison. He's known her longer than I have. I have nothing to offer."

"That's not true," said Vincent. "Winlaw can take his frustration out on you. Give Daxton your keys."

Cody reached into his pocket and took out a key ring. He tried to remove the car key, but his hands were trembling and he couldn't get it off the ring.

"Just give him the whole set," said Vincent. "Getting locked out of your house is the least of your worries right now."

Cody handed over the keys. Daxton was having a very, very bad day, but Cody's was probably going to be worse. Daxton honestly felt a little bit sorry for that poor son of a bitch.

He couldn't think of any savage parting words, so he just silently left through the front door.

As he walked toward Cody's car, he took out his cell phone. He'd missed several calls from Winlaw. Presumably, when Winlaw ripped out Daxton's tenth toenail, he'd say, "*And that was for ignoring my calls!*"

He got into Cody's car, backed out of the driveway, and sped off.

It wasn't like Winlaw had the resources to place roadblocks

around the city. If Daxton drove all day and all night, stopping only to refuel, and then went to live in a cabin for a few months, Winlaw might forget about his vendetta. Maggie would bitch about it all day, every day, but at least she'd be alive. And it would be a good story for their kid.

A few minutes later, another call from Winlaw came through. Daxton ignored it.

Then a text message.

You're digging yourself in deeper.

Winlaw despised text messages. This was really serious.

Another text: *I know you're seeing these.*

There really wasn't anything Daxton could do to plead his case. He didn't respond.

How much worse are you trying to make this for yourself?

How much worse could it get?

And then a picture. Daxton slammed on the brakes as he saw the image of Maggie, one eye swollen, duct tape over her mouth.

Shall we trade?

Daxton screamed and slammed his fists against the steering wheel. He screamed in frustration, and he screamed in misery, and he screamed in horror, all while he pounded the steering wheel until his hands felt like they were broken. He resisted the urge to smash them against the windows.

Daxton...?

No. They weren't going to trade. He wasn't going to give his life for Maggie's.

He wanted to fling the phone to the floor and stomp on it until it shattered, but no. He'd need it. He had to be smart about this. He tossed the phone into the back seat instead.

He wondered if Winlaw would tell Maggie that Daxton had

refused to come back for her. Stupid question. Of course he would. He'd taunt her with the knowledge that Daxton didn't love her or their child enough to sacrifice himself for them.

That would hurt worse than when he took out the tools.

No, it wouldn't. Once he went to work on her, she'd forget all about Daxton and anything else but the pain.

Daxton looked at himself in the rearview mirror. That was what a cowardly piece of shit looked like. But no amount of self-loathing was going to get him to give himself up. He'd warned Maggie that she was in danger. She obviously hadn't taken him seriously enough.

He resumed driving.

18

Spiral was not a good car passenger. He kept pacing and meowing and climbing all over Allison and jumping down dangerously close to the gas and brake pedals. When she brought him home from the animal shelter, he'd slept most of the way, but she'd been calm and soothing and he was probably happy to get out of the cage. Now she was a nervous wreck, and the cat was appropriately stressed out.

She was driving seventy-four miles per hour on a sixty-five miles-per-hour highway, since as long as she wasn't exceeding the speed limit by ten miles per hour she was unlikely to get pulled over. She'd been driving for about thirty minutes, and still had no thoughts as to where she should go, besides "far away." Her thoughts were consumed by images of the people she'd killed.

And then Allison noticed red and blue flashing lights in her rearview mirror. Oh, God. Had the police found the bodies? Did the authorities have an APB out for her car?

She glanced at the speedometer. Shit. She was actually going quite a bit faster than seventy-four. How long had she been doing that without noticing?

She didn't trust herself to outrun the cops in a high-speed pursuit, so she applied the brakes and pulled over to the side. She took a long, deep breath. Stay calm. Nothing to worry about. It was just a speeding ticket. She'd be fine.

But now she was second-guessing the effectiveness of her shower. It had been way too quick. She'd missed some blood for sure. Maybe there was blood on her ear or in her hair. She didn't want the cop to catch her checking out her reflection—he'd think she was wondering if her eyes were dilated or something like that—so she stared straight ahead, trying desperately to stay calm, but desperation was the opposite of calmness.

What if she killed a cop?

She couldn't even simply accept defeat and turn herself in. She could kill him from the back of the police car while handcuffed. If she tried to explain this to him, he'd think she was lying or insane.

The only way this wouldn't end horribly was if she could stay calm.

Nice and calm. Respectful and polite.

A speeding ticket was no big deal. That might be all this was about. Maybe he'd even let her off with a warning. She'd apologize and be on her way.

Calm. Very calm. Not calm enough that he thought she'd just taken a hit of marijuana, but calm.

The police officer got out of his vehicle. He was a big guy. Military haircut. No-nonsense stride to his walk. Allison rolled down her window as he approached.

He leaned down. "License, registration, and proof of

insurance." He was scowling, but she wasn't sure if he was angry, or if his face just naturally formed a scowl. He kind of gave off the vibe of somebody who scowled even when he wasn't upset.

Allison opened the glove compartment, took out her registration, and handed it to him. Spiral jumped onto her lap as she unzipped her purse. She found her driver's license right away. She knew her proof of insurance was in here, but she wasn't completely sure where, so she began to rifle through the contents.

Stay calm. Everything is fine. You'll find it. It's no big deal. Just a traffic stop.

Could he tell how nervous she was?

Of course he could.

So what? Everybody was nervous when they got pulled over by a cop. It would be weird for her *not* to be nervous.

"I'm sorry," she said. "I know it's in here."

"Not a problem," said the cop. His words were friendly but his tone said, "*If you pull a gun out of your purse, I promise you won't have a chance to shoot it.*"

It was fine. Perfectly fine. She'd been speeding. He had no clue that anything else had happened today.

"May I ask what this is about?"

"Find your proof of insurance first, please."

"Yes, yes, of course."

Where the hell was it?

Calm down. Don't panic.

"If you don't have the paperwork, you can probably pull it up on your phone," the cop told her.

"Thank you," said Allison. "I don't actually have my phone with me right now."

"You don't have your phone?"

"No, I—" She almost said "*left the house in a hurry*" but that would be a terrible answer. "I'm forty-five years old. I still remember pay phones. I have a cell phone, obviously, but I don't have it glued to my hand like kids do these days."

"They come in useful when you can't find your insurance card," the cop said.

"Right. They do. I'm sorry." Allison continued digging through her purse.

Seriously, where the fuck was the paperwork? She hadn't thrown it away. The only possible place it could be was in her purse, and it wasn't as if her purse was in complete disarray.

She couldn't find it because she was getting frantic.

"What happens if I can't find it?" she asked.

"Are you done looking?"

"Not yet."

She found a small folded piece of paper. Was this it? Yes! She breathed a sigh of relief and handed it to the cop. He quickly glanced at it and nodded.

"Do you know how fast you were going?" the cop asked.

"Yes, sir."

"And do you know the speed limit on this highway?"

"Yes, sir, I do. I'm sorry."

"Eighty-one miles per hour is considered reckless driving."

The cop's scowl intensified. He rubbed his forehead as if struck by a sudden migraine. He removed his hand then seemed to be making a conscious effort to regain his focus.

"I didn't know that, sir," said Allison, her voice quivering a bit.

Calm down calm down calm down calm down...

"Reckless driving is a..." The cop trailed off, as if he lost his train of thought.

What could she do?

A thin trickle of blood ran from his nostril. The cop wiped it away with the back of his index finger. He looked at his finger, then returned his attention to Allison.

"Reckless driving is..."

His other nostril began to bleed.

Should she confess everything? Explain to him that she had telekinetic powers, which is what was making his nose bleed, and that he needed to return to his vehicle immediately? What if he actually believed her? It would save his life.

"Sir, I—"

The cop waved at her to stop talking. "I'm going to run your plates. I'll be right back."

Allison watched in the rearview mirror as he returned to his car, walking like somebody in extreme pain.

He opened the door but didn't get inside.

He stood there for a few seconds.

Then he closed the door again and walked back over to her.

The cop handed Allison her license, registration, and insurance paper. "I'm going to let you off with a warning," he said. "Watch your speed."

"I will. Thank you."

She rolled her window back up as the cop left. Oh, thank freaking God. She started the engine and resumed her drive.

At some point soon she'd have to pull over and try to send a message to Cody to tell him not to come over. She had the dead guy's phone, and though she didn't know Cody's phone number or e-mail address, it couldn't be that difficult to track them down, or at least look him up on social media. But he'd still be at work, so her top priority was to put as much distance as she could between herself and the additional people who might want to kill her.

She'd turned off Location Services on the phone, so in theory they shouldn't be able to use it to find her. As soon as she got a replacement she'd destroy this one.

About half an hour later, the phone rang. Boss Man.

"Hello?" she answered.

"It's done," said Winlaw.

"That was quick."

"They work efficiently. This took quite a bit longer than usual, but there were a lot of bodies."

"Well, thank you," said Allison. "I appreciate it."

"Would you be interested in meeting in person?"

"Are you asking me out?"

"Excuse me?" said Winlaw.

"I was kidding."

"Oh. Very good. It's not often that somebody can catch me off-guard like that. I knew I liked you. But, no, I'm not asking you out. I'd like to discuss your special gifts and how they can be mutually beneficial."

"I'm sure that will be a very interesting discussion," said

Allison. "I'm all in favor of it, but I'm going to lay low for a while. I'm sure you understand."

"I can protect you."

"Well, sure you can. I mean, you're the one who's trying to have me killed. Or captured, or whatever it is you want. I'm not that impressed that you can protect me from yourself."

"What I meant was that I'll make sure nobody else comes after you, and I can make sure nobody finds out about the bodies."

"Great," said Allison. "That's good to hear. I'm still going to lay low for a while, if you don't mind. Maybe a day or two. Let's say one day. Twenty-four hours. Give me twenty-four hours to make sure my house isn't on the national news, and we'll work out some kind of meet and greet. Sound okay?"

"It doesn't sound like I have a choice."

"You don't. I'm glad you understand that. I'll give you a call tomorrow, I promise."

"All right." His tone was not that of somebody who thought it was all right.

Allison hung up. In twenty-four hours, she'd be halfway across the country, and Winlaw could go fuck himself.

19

Somebody started the van's engine. Cody couldn't see who, since he was tied up in the back, with a sack over his head. Well, technically he wasn't tied up—they'd used duct tape. Lots and lots of duct tape.

While the younger one wrapped the tape around his hands and feet, the older one had kicked Cody and told him to stop struggling. He hadn't been struggling. He was, in fact, being as polite and cooperative as he possibly could. Obviously, the older one just wanted to kick him.

After they taped his mouth, put the sack over his head, and tossed him into the back of the van, not gently, Cody had lain there, trying to figure out how he was going to escape. The sliding door on the side of the van kept opening every minute or so, and there'd be the thump of something heavy being tossed inside, presumably a full body bag.

He tried not to think about the fact that he was sharing a van with corpses.

The list of strange things that Cody was willing to believe existed did *not* include zombies, so he'd be fine. The dead bodies couldn't hurt him. He couldn't see them or smell them. All he had to worry about was joining their ranks—which, if he needed to justify his current anxiety level, was a pretty damn legitimate concern.

So now they were driving away from Allison's house.

They hit quite a few bumps. Cody wondered how he'd react if the body bags slid toward him. Poorly, he assumed.

They'd taken away his cell phone and he couldn't see anything anyway, so he wasn't sure how long the ride lasted. Definitely not as long as it felt, since that was approximately a million years.

The van stopped.

The rear doors opened and a couple of people lifted Cody up by his hands and feet. They said nothing as they carried him. Their footsteps sounded like they were on cement, then a door opened, then it sounded like they were on carpet.

They dropped him onto the floor.

"*Gentle,*" a man said. "That's no way to treat our guest."

At least three people laughed at that witticism.

"Can you hear me?" the man asked.

Cody nodded.

"I'm going to remove the hood. Are you going to behave?"

Cody nodded again.

"Do I have to spell out what will happen if you fail to behave?"

Cody shook his head.

Somebody removed the sack. The bright light stung Cody's eyes and he squeezed them shut.

"That's fine, let your eyes adjust," said the man. "We're in no hurry here."

Cody slowly opened his eyes. He was in a small, fairly unimpressive office. He'd expected something more opulent from a guy who could send men off to their deaths.

The older guy on the cleanup crew was in the room but not the younger one. He stood off to the side, next to a man who looked about thirty but whose facial hair looked like a teenage boy trying to grow his first mustache. The man speaking to Cody was middle-aged, wore a rumpled suit, and looked like a raging asshole.

"You must be Cody," said the man. He tore the duct tape off Cody's mouth, making no effort not to remove skin in the process.

"Yeah."

"I'm Dominick Winlaw."

"Hey, how's it going?"

"It's been an interesting day. More casualties than I would've expected when I woke up this morning."

"I know, right?"

"You're not doing a very good job of pretending that you're not terrified," said Winlaw.

"I'm not ashamed of that," said Cody.

"We're going to play a little game called Prove Your Usefulness. The way it works is, you're going to prove that it's worth it for me to keep you around, or I slash your throat. It may seem like a quick and relatively painless death, but I assure you, choking on your own blood is an awful way to go."

Cody nodded. "You really didn't have to sell me on the idea that having my throat slashed would suck."

"Do you know Allison Teal?"

"Yes."

"Do you know where to find her?"

"Right now? No. I've been in a van with a bag over my head."

Winlaw smiled. "I like you. But I don't like you enough to spare your life if you bring nothing of value. So focus less on trying to be charming and more on letting me know what you can offer."

"I really wasn't trying to be charming," said Cody. "Any chance you could cut the tape off my hands and feet?"

"No."

"It's awkward to have a conversation when all I can do is flop around on the floor. C'mon, there are three of you. Where am I gonna go?"

"I didn't get to where I am by cutting people free before they'd earned it."

"That's fair, I guess. I just figured that a goodwill gesture on your part would help with the negotiations."

"You figured wrong," said Winlaw. "My goodwill gesture is that your throat doesn't have a huge red gash across it. That's not going to last much longer. In fact, I'm done with you. Matt, open up his throat."

The older guy from the cleanup crew reached into his pocket, took out a switchblade knife, and snapped out the blade.

"Okay, okay," said Cody. "I can help you find her."

Winlaw looked over at Matt. "I didn't tell you to stop."

Matt crouched down next to Cody, who frantically tried to scoot away even though it was ridiculous to think that he could get away. "Seriously! I can help! I'll behave."

"You're acting like we're equals, and that is most definitely not the case," said Winlaw. "I'm going to dissuade you from that notion."

"I'm dissuaded," Cody insisted.

"Cut his throat a little," Winlaw told Matt. "Make it bleed but don't make it spew blood all over the place. I still want him to be able to answer questions."

"No! Please! I apologize! I really apologize!"

"I recommend that you lie still," said Winlaw. "He's very good at slitting throats, but if you keep squirming he might cut deeper than he intends to. Close your eyes, lie there, and take it."

Cody decided that further pleading would indeed be the end of him. He closed his eyes and tensed up his entire body, praying that it was a bluff. Matt would press the blade against his neck, hold it there for a moment, then pull it away, followed by a warning that the next time he wouldn't get off so easy.

He felt the tip of the blade press into his neck, just under his jawbone, not breaking the skin.

Then it broke the skin.

Cody let out a whimper as the blade slowly moved. It didn't feel like Matt was cutting deep but it hurt like hell. His instincts were to pull away, but he forced himself to remain perfectly still.

After making about an inch-long cut, Matt pulled the knife away.

"You can open your eyes again," said Winlaw. "He's done."

Cody wanted to just start weeping, but he didn't. He opened his eyes.

"You'll get one more chance after this," Winlaw informed him. "He'll do the same thing, but to your dick. Unless genital mutilation is your kink, I'd advise you to cooperate."

"I will. I completely will." Cody tried to sit up but couldn't. "Like I told Daxton—"

"You talked to Daxton?"

"Yes."

"Interesting. Please continue."

"Like I told him, I have no loyalty to Allison," Cody lied. "I barely know her. We had one date, and it was barely a date. We didn't even kiss. There were no sparks at all, but even if there *were* sparks, I saw what she did to your men. Maybe she was defending herself and maybe she wasn't, but I will never get that image out of my brain. It's not safe for her to be out there. Who knows who she'll do this to next? Maybe she'll kill a little kid."

"You're making a case for why you're on my side, but not for how you can help me."

"We had a second date planned. I was going to her house after work. As far as she knows, I think it's still on. She won't want me showing up there or getting worried and calling the police, so she'll find a way to get in touch with me."

This part was all true, of course, since he didn't want to get caught in a lie. He wasn't yet sure how he'd eventually turn this against Winlaw and his men, but he'd figure something out. He sure as hell wasn't going to lure Allison into a trap. He'd die before he did that. He didn't want to die, but he wasn't as devoted to staying alive as they might think.

"Does she know your number?" asked Winlaw.

"Yes."

"Even if she doesn't have her phone?"

"Maybe. I'm not hard to track down. She could Google me pretty easily, I'd think."

Winlaw extended his hand toward Matt. "Let me have his phone."

Matt took Cody's cell phone out of his pocket and gave it to him.

"What's your passcode?" Winlaw asked.

"I don't have one."

"You don't?" Winlaw tapped the screen. "You sure don't. Why would you not have a passcode?"

"I just never set one up."

"What if your phone got stolen?"

"I'd want them to figure out who I was so they could return it."

"What about your banking information?"

"I don't do anything like that on my phone. I mostly just use it for games."

"Can you believe that?" Winlaw asked the other men in the room. "Leaves his phone unlocked. That's insane."

"I could put one on now."

"Let me see," said Winlaw, swiping away at the screen. "Yep, you did call her. That's good. Don't get many calls, do you?"

"No."

"Not many text messages, either. It doesn't look like you're a very popular fellow, Cody. Well, let's see what you and Allison texted about. You were worried about her. You didn't think she sounded okay. You're a pretty good friend for somebody you just met. Trying to get a little bit of action, were you?"

"Not on the second date."

"Third date rule. That's right. Good for you for being a gentleman." Winlaw set the phone on his desk. "Did she say anything about any kind of interesting and unusual abilities she might have?"

"What do you mean?"

"You know what I mean."

"In bed?"

"I mean, telekinetic powers."

"Are you asking me if Allison is psychic?"

"Psychic isn't the same thing. At least I don't think it is. Apparently your friend can do amazing things with her mind, like murdering several of my employees."

"You think she did that with her mind?"

"You saw the bodies. How do you think she did it?"

"Well, I certainly didn't think she did that with her mind," said Cody. "There were stab wounds and burn marks and stuff. I figured she was savage with a knife. Is that seriously why I'm here? Because you think she's some sort of witch?"

"For all I know, she's a ninja. I just wanted your perspective."

"No, she never said anything to me about sorcery."

"All right." Winlaw smiled. "Congratulations. You've convinced me that it's worth keeping you alive for a while longer. I can fake a text, but not a phone call or your face on video chat, so I'm not going to kill you right now."

"Thank you."

"Put him in storage," Winlaw told the other men.

They picked up Cody and carried him out of the office and down a short hallway. Matt let the top half of Cody drop as he opened a door. He picked Cody up again, and they tossed him into the room, slamming the door shut as soon as he struck the floor.

Cody was in a very small room, about the size of a handicapped stall in a restroom. The walls were bare.

He wasn't alone.

"Hi," he said to the pregnant woman.

"Hi."

"I see that you're still pregnant."

"Yeah."

"Hmmm. I'd heard differently."

"It was a con."

"I'm Cody."

"Maggie."

"Did somebody punch you, or did you get that black eye by accidentally bumping into something?"

"Somebody punched me."

"You have to be a real piece of shit to punch an expectant mother."

"Yeah."

"You also have to be a real piece of shit to make somebody think that she killed your baby."

"It wasn't my idea."

"Daxton's?"

"None of your business."

"We'll go with Daxton. I wasn't real impressed with his moral compass when we hung out."

"Whatever."

"Do you want to, I don't know, join forces? I'm scrawny and you're pregnant and we're both duct-taped up, but there are two of us now. Three, technically."

"What's the baby going to do for us?" Maggie asked.

"Nothing," said Cody. "It was just something to say. I'm not trying to imply that we aren't utterly screwed, but if we work together we're a little less screwed, right?"

"If you say so."

"The logic holds up."

"Daxton was supposed to be here by now. They're going to kill me—slowly—if he doesn't give himself up. It looks like he's just going to leave me to die. So forgive me if I don't have bright hopes for the future right now."

"Maybe he's stuck in traffic."

Maggie glared at him. "Go to hell."

"I'm sure he'll do the right thing."

"And I'm sure he won't."

"Can you at least promise me that if an opportunity comes up to escape, we'll take advantage of it?"

Maggie shrugged. "Sure."

The door opened.

"I need to take your picture," Matt told Cody.

"Okay."

"The problem is that except for the cut on your neck, you look pretty good. I need you to look bad. So I'm going to kick you in the face a couple of times, maybe three, so that you look right for your photo op."

Cody didn't protest. He just braced himself for the pain.

Having never been kicked in the face, Cody found that the pain was quite a bit worse than he expected, and his expectations had been high.

"Good job," said Matt. "You sure how know to take a kick. I'm going to give it a few minutes for the swelling to really look nice, and then I'll be back to take your picture. You're on Facebook, right? You can have a new profile pic."

Cody just lay there for those few minutes. Maggie said nothing.

Matt returned, took Cody's picture, and then closed the door, chuckling.

20

The exit sign for the next town showed that they had several fast food restaurants and hotels, so hopefully they'd have a library as well. Allison didn't think she could safely enable the Internet on this cell phone, but if she used a public computer to send a message to Cody, it shouldn't tag her location.

She didn't know that for sure. It might. Somebody proficient with such things might be able to trace where she'd sent the message from, but she'd take the risk in order to make sure that Cody knew she was cancelling their get-together. If she ghosted him, he might head over there after work anyway. He might decide that she simply wasn't home, or he might call 911 and report her as a possible suicide. In theory, if the police broke down her door they'd find nothing of interest inside, but she had no reason to believe that she could completely trust Winlaw's cleaning crew. Best to just keep Cody away.

She took the exit. If she was lucky, she'd be able to find a library, or a sign directing her to one, by just driving down the main street.

The phone rang. Winlaw again.

Allison didn't want to answer but she probably shouldn't ignore him. She touched the screen to accept the call. "Yeah?"

"Hi, Allison," said Winlaw.

"I said I needed twenty-four hours. If you're going to harass me, I don't know how we can work together."

"I apologize. Shall I hang up?"

"No, just tell me why you called."

"What are you doing right now?"

"I'm driving."

"You should pull over."

"Why?"

"Because you're about to become very upset, and I don't want you to get into an accident."

Allison pulled into the parking lot of a furniture store. She parked in the spot furthest from the store but left the engine on. "What did you want to tell me?"

A text message popped up. It contained a picture of Cody. His face looked like somebody had beaten the shit out of him.

"Did you get it?" Winlaw asked.

"Yes."

"Doesn't look very good, does he?"

"Tell me what you want me to do."

"I want to meet with you."

"I hardly know him," Allison said. "He's a nice enough guy, but he doesn't mean anything to me."

"Yeah, he said you weren't close. I figure it's win-win for me. Either he gives you the incentive to return home, or I get to enjoy my hobby of making people scream. There's no time limit. You want to wait a few weeks? That's fine. Cody will still be alive, even though he'll wish he wasn't."

"Let me talk to him."

"No."

"I'm not coming back if I can't talk to him."

"He'll be very disappointed to hear that."

"How do I know he isn't already dead?"

"Well, Allison, I guess you'll just have to trust that I'm not staring at his severed head right now, with its lifeless, glassy eyes. It took a while. The blade wasn't very sharp."

"I'll fucking kill you."

"Oh, no, no, no, let's not go there. Let's keep this civil. I'm kidding about his head, of course. I haven't killed him yet. And I wouldn't expect you to trust me without hearing his melodic voice. So I'm going to open the door to his cage—don't worry, it's not really a cage—and let him speak to you."

Allison felt like she could crush the phone in her fist as she waited.

"Say something to Allison," Winlaw said, not speaking directly into the phone.

Cody was almost shouting when he said: "It was a lie! The baby's fine! I'm with the mother right now!"

"All right, that's enough," said Winlaw into the phone. Allison heard a door close. "Is that enough proof? Or do you want to listen to me saw one of his toes off?"

"I believe you."

Allison's mind was reeling in two completely different directions. They'd kidnapped Cody. They were going to murder him if she didn't return. But the baby was a lie! All of that anguish over a lie! She wasn't sure how to process both emotions at once.

"How far are you from home?" Winlaw asked.

"A couple of hours."

"That's disappointing. I hoped you were closer. So you just sped right off, huh?"

"Yes."

"Well, you can just speed right on back home. And you're going to do me a little favor. When we're done with this call, you're going to go into Settings on the phone, and then Privacy, and then you're going to turn Location Services back on. It's how I track my employees, and you basically work for me now. If you don't answer a call, I'll have to assume that you ditched the phone, and then I will be very angry. I can't take my anger out on you, so...well, you know how this is going to play out."

"I won't ditch the phone," said Allison.

"I'll give you a meeting place when you get closer. Do you have any questions?"

"No."

"Good. Drive safely."

Winlaw hung up. Allison just stared at the phone in her hand.

She needed to get back on the road. Not simply to follow Winlaw's instructions—if somebody happened to walk by her parked car while she was in this emotional state, their skull would probably burst apart.

She drove out of the parking lot.

She didn't *have* to change her plan. She didn't have to turn back. She could throw the phone out the window and keep on driving as before. Why should she put her life in danger for a guy she'd just met? They'd shared some secrets, had a nice dinner, and they worked on a jigsaw puzzle together. That was all.

Why was she bothering to pretend that she might abandon him?

She wasn't going to leave Cody to die. She wasn't going to trade one source of nightmarish guilt for another. Even if he was a complete stranger, she wouldn't let Winlaw murder somebody because of her.

Cody had been trying to help her. And she was going to help him.

She wasn't going to surrender. She wasn't going to negotiate.

No, she was going to kill Winlaw. And if anybody else stood in her way as she rescued Cody, she'd kill them, too.

She hoped they *did* stand in her way.

Rivers of blood. Piles of broken bones.

Allison was coming for them.

21

After filling up his gas tank, Daxton decided to check to see how many enraged calls he'd missed from Winlaw. He opened the back door, picked up his cell phone, and glanced at the screen. Only two. Plus a text message.

I'm offering you an extension if you call ASAP.

That seemed very much unlike Winlaw, but he couldn't torture Daxton to death through the phone, so he might as well return the call.

Winlaw picked up immediately. "My offer had almost expired."

"Let me talk to Maggie."

"No. She's still alive, but it doesn't matter to me if you believe me or not. I'd like to make you a deal. Information in exchange for a twenty-four hour extension on your deadline to turn yourself in."

"What kind of information?"

"I want to know exactly what Allison looks like, and what kind of car she's driving."

Daxton had no intention of turning himself in, but there was a very strong appeal to the idea of having twenty-four more hours before Winlaw tried to hunt him down. "Sure, I can tell you that, no problem."

DOMINICK WINLAW DIDN'T HAVE an army of highly trained assassins at his disposal. He had a few guys who he could use for more dangerous jobs—most of whom were dead now—and the rest of the people who worked for him were mostly lowlifes. Drug dealers, pimps, and thieves weren't going to stop somebody like Allison...unless he had a *lot* of them. All hands on deck. She could kill a few men who rushed into her own home, but she couldn't kill five times that many, when they were ready for her.

A couple of his men were making the calls. Gathering as many people as they could. He couldn't bring them all here, since there might be gunfire and screaming, but there was a campground, closed for the season, that he could use. He was friends with the owner, and the noise level would not be a problem.

If he was lucky, bringing everybody to the campground would be an unnecessary effort. There were multiple parts to his plan, and now that he had two men headed out to intercept her, this might be over before she even made it back to town. He'd tell everybody at the campground that it was a surprise party. He should send somebody out for lots of beer, just in case.

Somebody knocked on his office door. It was the timid

knock of Karl, who jokingly called himself Winlaw's secretary. Technically he did perform many of the duties of an administrative assistant, but Winlaw thought of him as more of a bodyguard.

"Come in."

Karl opened the door. He was a huge guy who looked like no secretary ever employed. "I know you didn't want to be bothered..."

"And yet you're doing it anyway."

"Well, it's Olivia."

Winlaw cursed under his breath. "Send her in."

A moment later, his daughter walked into his office. Her eyes were puffy from crying and her mascara was streaked. Since she'd spent the past couple of weeks crying, it was pretty clear that she kept wearing mascara to emphasize the fact that she was doing all of this crying, just in case Winlaw wasn't paying attention.

She closed the door behind her and sat in front of his desk.

"I can't do this anymore," she said.

By "this" she meant pretend that she believed the story that Sam had gotten cold feet about their marriage and left town. Her timing might seem to be bad, except that she'd said this almost every night since her fiancé "went missing," and Winlaw had always been able to talk her down.

"All right," said Winlaw. "What are you going to do?"

"I want to know what *you* are going to do. I know he's dead, and I know he's dead because of you. What are you going to do about it?"

The same conversation. He'd insist that he had no idea what happened to Sam, and she'd scream and curse at him, while also being careful not to step too far out of line and risk causing a rift between her and a father who paid all of her bills. The conversation broke Winlaw's heart every time. He wished there was something he could do, but he knew Sam wasn't coming back. Vincent and Matt had shown him a picture of Sam's body, taken when they cleaned up the mess.

Maybe he could change the conversation this time.

"I'm working on it right now," he said.

"You are?"

Winlaw nodded. "You remember Daxton Sink, right?"

"Yeah. He's always staring at my ass."

"Sam's death was his fault."

Olivia lowered her eyes. "So he *is* dead."

"You already knew that."

"Daxton killed him?"

"No, he got him killed through negligence. Sam got shot in the head, so it was quick and painless. Daxton is on the run, but we'll catch him, I promise."

"And when you do...?"

"What would you like to happen?"

"I'd like to spend some time alone with him."

Winlaw smiled. "That can be arranged."

ALLISON NEEDED A BETTER plan than "kill them all."

She couldn't think of one, though.

She'd been driving for about an hour now, and Winlaw had indeed called a few times to make sure she answered. Once he called within thirty seconds of the previous call, just to make sure she didn't think she had a window of opportunity. She didn't know how well he could pinpoint her location, but for Cody's sake, she had to assume that he could tell if she stopped to buy machine guns and ammunition.

She had ten thousand dollars in her bug-out bag. She was toying with the idea of bribing somebody to go get weapons for her. This plan would require her to stop long enough to find a Good Samaritan, and then stop to meet up with them later. It also required her to be a good enough judge of character to pick somebody who wouldn't speed off with her cash or report her to the authorities. It wasn't much of a plan. She probably wouldn't do it.

Winlaw, knowing what she could do, would take precautions.

And if Allison went on a murderous rampage, how could she be sure she wouldn't find a broken, dead Cody at the end of it?

For now, her plan remained "kill them all."

WINLAW SAT up straight as his phone vibrated. The incoming call was from Buster Dreys.

Buster was a skilled employee, a jack-of-all-trades. Valuable enough that Winlaw didn't kill him for skimming off the top of some of his cash deliveries, or helping himself to a bit of the merchandise when running drugs. He'd let it go for a while, since the amounts were too small to impact his bottom line, but then he decided that he didn't like the idea of Buster thinking he was pulling one over on his boss. Winlaw had calmly but firmly told him not to ever steal from him again. Buster had promised that there would never be another incident, and then he literally shit his pants.

"We found her," said Buster.

"Are you serious?"

"Unless there's another black-haired middle-aged woman driving a silver Prius V where the GPS says her phone is transmitting from, yeah, we're on her. I'm right behind her now. Paul and I will trade off so she doesn't get suspicious."

"Don't lose her."

"We won't."

"Hold steady. She may need to stop for gas."

"We can't just nab her at a gas station, can we?"

"Not in front of a dozen witnesses, no. Look for an opportunity. Don't get impatient. Don't take any unnecessary risks. If you have to follow her all the way back here, that's fine. Do your best."

"We will. I'll keep you posted."

Winlaw hung up. In theory, he could call up Allison and instruct her to follow one of their cars, and have them lead her someplace secluded. But then she'd be on high alert. He needed her to have no idea that people were after her already. This first phase was all about the element of surprise.

Time to give Allison another call.

"Hi, asshole," she answered.

"Just checking in."

"I know."

"Looks like you're making good time."

"Yep."

"I'll call you later."

"I'll be waiting, asshole."

Winlaw hung up. He was happy to let Allison call him an asshole if it made her feel better, though if she ended up in his employ her attitude would change *very* quickly.

IT HAD BEEN ABOUT twenty minutes since they last spoke, and if Winlaw didn't call in the next five minutes, Allison was going to call him.

As soon as she made this decision, he called.

"Hey," she said, deciding to skip the "asshole" part this time. "You've gotta let me stop at a rest area or my bladder's going to explode. I'll be quick, I promise."

"You can have ten minutes," said Winlaw. "Not a second more."

"Thank you."

"SHE'S GOING to stop at the next rest area," Winlaw told Buster. "Which of you is behind her right now?"

"Dean is. I'm maybe a quarter-mile ahead."

"Perfect. I told her she could have ten minutes, so she may linger. See if you can make anything happen. Only do it if it's completely safe. No risks."

"Will do."

Buster parked in the rest area. It wasn't crowded, but nor was it barren. There were plenty of possible witnesses around.

He opened the glove compartment and took out the rag and the small bottle of Chloroform. As he did this, Allison parked a few spaces away from him. Dean pulled up right next to him.

Allison got out of her car and quickly hurried toward the restrooms, moving like somebody who really, really had to pee.

Buster left the bottle and rag on the seat as he and Dean got out of their vehicles. He glanced around to make sure nobody was close enough to overhear them. "What do you think?"

Dean looked around. "I don't like it."

"We might not get another chance."

"He said not to worry if we couldn't catch her. He said not to take any risks."

"That is indeed what he said," Buster agreed.

"You think he'll be pissed if we miss this chance?"

"I think he'll be happier if we don't miss it."

"How do we pull this off? We can't just tackle her and drag her to the car."

"We just need an opportunity to get the rag over her mouth without anybody seeing. We need, like, a five second window."

"Do you think we can get five seconds?" Dean asked.

"We should at least try."

"All right. Let's do it."

Buster got back into his car and poured some Chloroform onto the rag. Then he neatly folded it up. Nobody would see him and think, "*Hey, that dude is holding a Chloroform-soaked cloth!*"

He got out of the car again, shut the door, then he and Dean walked toward the restrooms. They passed a couple of people, but nobody seemed suspicious of them.

There were a couple of teenagers in the vending machine area. If they turned around, they'd see the door to the women's restroom. But the angle wasn't right and they wouldn't see Buster or Dean reflected in the glass.

If Allison let out a gasp, they'd turn around.

As long as those teenagers were there, it wasn't safe to try to drug her. But this was the only place in the rest area that had enough cover. When she walked away from the building there'd be too many people around and they'd have to abandon the plan.

"Should we go in?" Dean asked.

"What if she's not the only one in there?"

"Then we apologize and step out. They'll think we're perverts or idiots."

"Y'know, they don't have urinals in there."

"You don't say. Are you saying that women don't have penises? Did I fall asleep that day in biology class?"

Buster glared at him. "What I'm saying is that they'll be in stalls, which means the doors will be closed, which means that if we move quick we can get her even if there are other people in there."

"I like it."

Buster looked back at the vending machines. What was taking those kids so damn long to choose? Just buy a can of soda and a candy bar and get the fuck out!

Through the door, Buster heard the air dryer turn on.

"If it's her, we do this. If it's not, we bail."

Dean nodded.

Buster pushed open the door.

Allison rubbed her hands under the dryer. Nobody in the history of human civilization had ever used one of these things until their hands were completely dry, and she would not be the one to break that streak.

Somebody walked into the restroom.

She wiped her hands off on her jeans.

She glanced over toward the door.

Two men were right next to her.

For a split-second she started to speak, to inform them that they'd accidentally gone into the wrong one, and then she realized that, no, these men were very much there on purpose.

One of them slammed a wet rag against her mouth.

22

Allison went limp in Buster's arms. He and Dean quickly led her out of the restroom. She was still partly walking on her own, like somebody who was completely drunk off their ass but hadn't lost all motor skills.

"It's all right, it's all right, we've got you," said Buster. The teenagers by the vending machines turned around to see what was going on. "She's a little lightheaded," Buster told them. "She'll be fine."

Several people stared as they led Allison to Dean's car, but as long as it looked like a low blood sugar episode and not a kidnapping, everything would work out.

"Do you want me to call an ambulance?" a woman asked as they passed her.

"No, no, that's not necessary at all. She's not supposed to skip any meals. We've got glucose tablets in the car."

Buster wished he'd had a few more seconds to really press the rag into Allison's face. He still had it, but even if he pretended that he was wiping off her mouth, it wouldn't be smart to try to give her another dose in front of all these people. She was barely conscious. They'd fix it once they got her into the car.

Almost there.

Allison's head slumped forward. Had she fallen asleep completely? That was good news if nobody at the rest area decided to interfere.

They got her to the car. Dean opened the passenger-side door and they got her inside, with everybody still watching. Buster fastened her seat belt, while they both reassured her and anybody who might overhear them that she was going to be totally fine.

Buster didn't have any pills on him. He had lots of them in the trunk—two crates—but going back to get them would not be intelligent. Instead, he mimed taking out a couple of pills and feeding them to her. It wasn't as if anybody was watching them through a telescopic lens. He picked up a bottle of water and tilted it to her lips.

"You follow me," he whispered to Dean.

Buster got in his own car. Considering that they nabbed Allison in broad daylight surrounded by witnesses, this had gone astoundingly well. They'd get out of the rest area, quickly find a spot without prying eyes, knock her out completely, and then throw her in the trunk.

She honestly seemed harmless. Buster had no idea why Winlaw was so concerned with capturing a middle-aged lady.

Allison hadn't been faking it. She'd been dizzy and loopy

and wanted nothing more than to curl up and go to sleep. She had to fight it.

One of the men who was trying to abduct her got into the driver's seat.

She didn't know if this was the best time to act. She did know that she wanted to escape long before he delivered her to Winlaw, and she also knew that she was safer fighting him now than when he was driving sixty-five miles per hour on the highway.

But she was so sleepy. It was hard to be scared and angry when she was so tired. It didn't help that she had to keep her eyes closed to make him feel like she posed no threat. If she could open them, it would be easier to stay awake.

Winlaw had Cody.

He was going to kill him.

She wasn't going to let Winlaw kill her friend.

Winlaw had to die.

Therefore, the driver of this car had to die.

Her anger was returning, far overpowering her fear. She tried to let it build up inside of her. Focus it inward. Fill herself with more and more rage until...

She opened her eyes and screamed.

The driver slammed his head into the steering wheel, honking the horn.

Then again. And again.

Allison assumed that this was drawing attention, but she didn't care. Nobody would see a guy bashing his face against the steering wheel and credit it to the passenger's telekinetic powers.

The steering wheel wasn't quite doing the trick. She needed

him to bash his skull against the dashboard. It was more solid and would do greater damage.

She tried to use her mind to adjust the trajectory of his head.

Instead, he tilted his head back. All the way back. Further than should've been physically possible.

His neck snapped.

His throat burst open.

He flopped forward.

In her peripheral vision she could see that the other guy was getting out of his car, so she didn't have much time. She quickly patted the dead man down. No gun. He had to have one somewhere, right?

She opened the glove compartment. There it was.

She grabbed the gun as the other man opened her door. She pointed it at his stomach. People in the rest area would know that some serious shit was going down, but she didn't think anybody was at the right angle to see her gun.

"Do you want to die?" she asked. Her words were slurred, but she thought he should be able to understand the question.

"No," he responded.

"I don't care if these..." She lost her train of thought for a second. "...if these people see me shoot you."

"I'll do whatever you want."

"Step away."

The man took a couple of big steps away from her. She shoved the gun into the waist of her jeans and got out of the car.

"We're going to my car," she told him.

"Mine's right here."

"Mine has my cat. Move fast. It's the silver Prius."

The man walked quickly toward Allison's car. She followed

him, close enough that she wouldn't miss if she shot him, but not so close that he could smack the gun out of her hand. She stumbled a couple of times but managed to stay upright.

People were watching them. One woman was on her phone. Allison couldn't worry about that right now.

They reached her car. She glanced through the window and saw that Spiral was asleep on the passenger's seat. She opened the door, picked the cat up with her free hand, and tossed him into the back seat as gently as possible. He'd forgive her. "Get in," she told the man.

The man obliged. Allison got in on the other side and turned on the engine.

"You try anything and I'll shoot you," she told him.

"I understand."

She backed out of her spot. Several people were watching her, and two men were hurrying toward the car with the fresh corpse. But nobody stood in her way or tried to stop her as she drove out of the rest area and back onto the highway.

"Take out your phone," she said. "Call your boss. Tell him that the plan went off without a hitch. Tell him that you're going to find someplace safe so you can tie me up and put me in the trunk. Deviate from that at all and I'll kill you." Allison was feeling much more alert.

"Okay."

"Repeat it back."

"The plan went off without a hitch. We're going someplace safe so I can—"

"So *we* can. Your partner is still alive, as far as he knows."

"We can tie you up and put you in the trunk."

"And then you tell him that you have to hang up."

The man nodded. "And then I'll tell him that I have to hang up."

"Call him. Put him on speaker. Don't fuck up."

The man took out his cell phone. It rang a couple of times, then she heard Winlaw's voice. "Hello?"

"Hi. This is Buster."

"I know who it is," said Winlaw. "How did it go?"

"Flawless. The plan went off without a hitch."

"Excellent. That's excellent."

"She's asleep in the back seat. We're going to take her someplace safe so we can wrap her in the tape and put her in the trunk."

"Perfect."

"Sorry if I sound weird. It was stressful. But we got it done."

Crap. He was overselling it.

"That's completely understandable," said Winlaw. "Keep me informed."

"I will. Gotta go." Buster hung up. "How was that?"

"Good job," Allison told him. "Thank you for not being stupid."

"Now what?"

"Now you hope that your boss isn't following the news that's happening sixty miles from home. Pretty sure your dead friend is going to get some press coverage."

"Now what besides that?"

"You're going to sit there and behave. You're now my bargaining chip."

Buster was not Allison's bargaining chip. She couldn't imagine that Winlaw had any real loyalty to him, not if he was sending Buster after somebody who'd killed a half-dozen of his other employees. Poor Buster was expendable as hell.

She had plans for him, but she wasn't going to share them yet, because he most definitely was not going to like them.

WINLAW WAS DELIGHTED by the news, but he wasn't willing to call off the rest of the operation until he had Allison in his possession. He might keep Cody alive a while longer to help control her. He'd execute Maggie with a bullet to the back of the head—he wasn't the kind of psychopath who would inflict pain upon a pregnant woman after she was no longer useful to him. Quick death. No pain, no fear.

ALLISON PULLED off at the next exit. She'd rather have put a little more distance between her and the rest area, but she didn't want Buster to get progressively braver.

She had no idea where she was going except "someplace secluded." She took random turns, trying to choose the path that seemed most likely to take her away from civilization.

"Where are we going?" Buster asked.

"Somewhere that I can put you in the trunk," she lied.

"You could do that here," he said. "Nobody's around. I'll jump right in."

She didn't respond and continued driving.

A few minutes later, she was satisfied. The dirt road was terrible to drive on—this was most definitely not a heavy-traffic route. She'd feel better if she reached a part where the road was impassable, but she still felt very confident that they wouldn't be interrupted.

She took the gun out of her waistband and held it up so Buster could see it. "Stay in the car until I tell you to get out."

Allison popped the trunk then got out of the vehicle. Her bug out bag had a roll of duct tape. She had not included it in her emergency supplies with the expectation that she'd use it to tape over somebody's mouth, but duct tape had an infinite number of uses.

She took out the roll of tape then closed the trunk.

"Now get out of the car," she told Buster.

Buster got out. He looked more suspicious than terrified. Clearly, she didn't need to go this far out of her way to safely move him to the trunk, but he didn't seem to realize yet that though he would indeed be going into the trunk, he wouldn't be alive when it happened.

She handed him the roll, since she couldn't unspool it and keep the gun pointed at him at the same time. "Tape your mouth shut. Do a good job. Wrap it around your head a few times."

"I'm one of Winlaw's top guys," Buster said. "He'll pay a lot to get me back."

"No, he won't. Tape your mouth."

Buster did as he was told, then he tore off the strip of tape and handed the roll back to her.

"Thank you," she said. "You've been very cooperative."

Buster nodded.

"I'm going to explain to you what's about to happen. I think that's only fair. Your boss wants me because I have powers that I can't really explain. That's how I broke your partner's neck. I don't know how I got them, and it's very difficult for me to control them. I've always wondered if they're like playing a musical instrument or a team sport. You can't get good at them right away."

Buster looked extremely confused.

"You've provided me with an opportunity I've never had before. And I'm going to make the most of it. Do you understand what I'm getting at?"

Buster shook his head.

"Thanks to you, I get to *practice*."

23

Now Buster looked terrified.

Allison was not going to get any pleasure from this. But nor was she going to wallow in guilt over what had to be done. If Buster didn't want to die an excruciatingly painful death, he shouldn't have tried to kidnap her.

Winlaw was presumably still tracking her phone and would wonder why they were stopped for so long. Let him wonder. She'd be in touch after this was over.

Wide-eyed, Buster backed up against the car. He made muffled noises that were clearly pleas for his life. Presumably he didn't know exactly what she meant by "practice," but he knew that it was going to turn out badly for him. She kept the gun pointed at him to discourage him from trying to run, though she had no intention of using a bullet on him.

It was a promising sign that Buster was still alive and unharmed. Allison wasn't feeling very calm, yet she hadn't accidentally broken any of his bones. She was already getting better at this.

She'd start by trying to break his leg. If she broke something higher up, he might decide to risk getting shot and just flee.

She stared at his leg, trying to focus specifically on the left one, to imagine the bone ripping through his flesh, poking through the fabric of his pants.

Nothing happened.

Buster clearly didn't understand what she was doing. His muffled tone now sounded like an attempt to negotiate.

She continued to focus on his leg, trying to harness all of her rage.

Nothing.

That was fine. That's why she was practicing.

Break, you shitty leg. Break in half. Shatter. Just the leg. Break into a million pieces. Spray fragments of bone everywhere. Break. Break. Break.

Buster let out a muffled cry of pain.

He fell completely back against the car but didn't topple over. He lifted his left leg as he whimpered.

If she'd broken his leg, he wouldn't be able to stand there like that. Had she broken his foot?

"I'm going to need you to take off your shoe," she told him. "Both of them. And your socks." Technically, she should make him strip naked so she could best see the impact of each of her experiments, but she wasn't quite prepared to ascend to that level of depravity.

Buster sat on the ground and obliged. He took off his right shoe and sock first, then yelped in pain as he took off the left. His big toe was bright red, though it hadn't yet begun to swell.

Now she'd try to break it worse.

She focused on the toe, imagining it breaking, creating a vivid picture in her mind of the toe twisting around until it popped right off his foot.

Twisting. Twisting. Twisting.

She moved her fingers as if twisting his toe off with them.

The toe twisted and snapped.

Buster's reaction was extremely loud. She probably should add a few more layers of duct tape before she broke him further.

She got the tape out of the car and wound it around the lower half of his face several more times, ignoring the pleading look in his eyes.

Back to work.

Now she wanted to break the toe next to it. She didn't know what the toe was called—the one that stayed home from the market.

She focused on twisting that particular toe, and moved her fingers again. Maybe that helped.

His toe twisted, but not the one she meant to break. It was the big toe again.

She tried to bend it upward.

The toe bent exactly as she intended.

The extra duct tape had been a good choice. Buster screamed and thrashed around in pain.

The hand gestures definitely helped. Instead of going for precision, she'd try to break his leg. She wasn't feeling as angry now, so she took a moment to remember that they'd kidnapped Cody. He was counting on her. They'd kicked him in the face, and they might be hurting him right now.

She concentrated on his left leg, then moved her hands as if snapping a branch over her knee.

His leg bent sideways and broke. A red splotch appeared near the knee of his pants.

It worked! She was learning how to control her ability! This could change her life!

She was ecstatic!

Buster's right arm broke.

Shit. She had to remember that strong positive emotions could have the same effect.

Focus.

Pinky finger on his right hand.

She concentrated and gestured.

His index finger began to bend.

Nope. *Pinky*. Focus.

His ring finger twitched.

Nope. Focus.

His pinky twitched. Began to bend backwards. Snapped.

Buster screamed. His eyes were wild, delirious with pain. She hoped he didn't pass out, and then she thought that it might be better if he did. Her abilities should still work, right?

Okay. What next? She'd flung Daxton across the room. She should try something like that with Buster. Toss him into the air.

Eight failed attempts and three accidental broken bones later, Buster left the ground. He went up a few feet and crashed down upon the trunk of the car, landing on his broken leg.

He tumbled off the car and lay still.

Allison knelt beside him. He was still breathing.

She tried to break the middle finger of his right hand. Got it on the first try.

Then she tried to break each of the toes on his left foot. She got three out of the five. On the second try, she broke the remaining two. She twisted his big toe over and over, like unscrewing the lid of a jar, until the skin split wide open.

It only took three tries to fling him into the air again.

Then only one.

She walked about a hundred feet away from him. Now she'd try for distance.

She tried to raise him into the air. Couldn't make it happen from this far away. Tried to break his arm. Couldn't do that, either.

She walked twenty paces closer and tried again.

No luck.

Fifty feet was still too far away.

Forty feet was too far.

Shit. She'd thought she could do it from this distance. She'd made Daxton's nose bleed from further than this, but she'd had to shriek to make it happen.

Buster let out an agonized moan. His fate was probably disproportionate to his crimes. He simply tried to kidnap the wrong woman at the wrong time, and now he was a *very* unfortunate guinea pig. Allison wished she felt worse about what she was doing to him.

She took one step at a time, trying to lift and break him after each one. Nothing was happening. It wasn't until she got about twenty feet away that his wrist bent back until it snapped. Buster shrieked beneath the duct tape. He was clearly not getting numb to all of the pain.

Allison could kill a man from twenty feet away. Good to know.

She didn't have much accuracy from that distance. An attempt to break his leg—in more places than she'd already broken it—broke his jaw instead. At least she thought she'd broken his jaw. The lower half of his face had given a violent jerk, but with all of the tape she couldn't be sure of the actual injury.

With her next move, his neck twisted, *Exorcist*-style. That wasn't her intention. He went silent.

She tried to lift him but nothing happened.

She walked right up to him and continued trying. No effect.

Okay. She couldn't do anything with dead people. No zombie army at her disposal.

Now she wished that she'd lifted him into the trunk while he was still barely alive. Or flung him off the side of the road. It was going to be difficult to get him into the trunk without help.

Actually, thanks to the situation at the rest area, the police might be looking for black-haired middle-aged women driving silver Prius V's. It probably wouldn't be such a great thing for her to have a dead body in her trunk. She didn't have nearly enough time to dig a shallow grave, but she'd drag Buster off the road and assume that nobody would find him for a while.

He'd suffered an awful death, but he'd given his life for scientific research, so in the end he'd brought some good into the world.

ALLISON AND SPIRAL had been back on the highway for a few minutes when Buster's cell phone buzzed.

Dominick Winlaw.

Allison decided not to answer it. Let that asshole wonder what was happening for a while longer.

WINLAW SLAMMED his phone down onto his desk. Of *course* it couldn't have been that easy. Of course not. Why had he ever imagined that it could be? He didn't know if Allison had somehow gotten the upper hand, or if Buster and Dean had some other reason for not answering his calls, but he had to assume that he'd be transitioning to the second phase of his plan.

It was time to move the captives to the campground. And almost everybody else.

He'd probably lose more men. If he counted Buster and Dean, and also Daxton, he now had nine fewer employees than he did before he'd heard of Allison. It wasn't as if he had a global operation with thousands of people working for him. She'd goddamn well better be worth it.

THE DOOR OPENED. Matt again. This time he was holding a gun.

"Time to get moving," he told Cody and Maggie, who were seated on the floor against the back wall.

"Where are we going?" Cody asked.

"Your graves, probably." Matt chuckled. "I'm just kidding. Our boss is obviously very stable. I'm sure he'll be able to work out a peaceful resolution to this whole thing."

ALLISON WAS HAVING good luck on the drive back. No cops, no traffic issues, and no tires falling off her car. She was close enough to home that it was time to answer the next time he called Buster, which he'd been doing every few minutes.

"Hi," she said, when he called.

"Allison."

"Was that a question?"

"No."

"Why do you keep calling? If Buster's phone ends up with the FBI, won't it seem suspicious that you've called him a dozen times?"

"That won't be a problem."

"I'm sure you've worked it all out. You seem very smart."

"What happened to Buster?"

"Oh, he's dead as fuck."

"I see."

"I mean, he's really, really dead. The other guy is dead, too, but he got off easy. Everybody you send after me ends up dead. I'm not telling you how to run your business, but I personally would stop sending people after me."

"Noted."

"We had a deal. You violated it. How can I trust you?" Allison asked.

"I understand why you're upset," said Winlaw. "To be fair, I never said I wouldn't send anybody after you. It's not my fault if you got that impression."

"Are you being serious right now?"

"I still have something you want. I will still kill Cody if you don't follow my instructions. I know you're feeling angry and homicidal right now, but don't forget who has the power here."

"Did Cody try to tell you we're soulmates or something? Maybe I care more about killing you than saving him."

"Do you?"

"I guess you'll find out."

"So is our negotiation over?"

"Not quite yet."

"I'm going to text you the address to a building. You'll park behind the building, and go through the unlocked back door into the garage. From there you'll get your next instructions."

"I don't want further instructions. I want to know where the fuck Cody is."

"And if you don't want the answer to that question to be that he's scattered in pieces all across town, you'll do what I say. Right now he's safe. He won't be safe if you forget who's calling the shots."

"All right," said Allison. "Send me the address. Is there anything left on your bucket list?"

"Why? Are you saying that I won't have a chance to complete them?"

"That's exactly what I'm saying. It didn't come out as clever as I'd intended, but yes, I'm saying that you're going to die tonight and never finish your bucket list."

"Maybe meeting you is on the list," said Winlaw.

"Is it the final item?"

"I guess we'll find out."

"Well, no, that's not how bucket lists work, but it doesn't matter. This conversation is becoming stupid. Send me the address."

24

Glenn and Rory were the sacrifices. Winlaw really didn't want any more of his men to perish, but he hoped it would be worth it in the end. The more of his men she killed, the more excited he was about the possibility of having her under his control.

Maybe Glenn and Rory would catch her. That would be great. Mostly, Winlaw was interested in watching the whole thing live, via the cameras that were already in the garage. He could see how exactly she killed them. Was it truly telekinetic powers, or was she just an insanely skilled assassin?

The cleanup of this mess was going to be a nightmare. If he'd known how much of a body count she'd rack up, he would've never sent the first wave of men to assist Daxton. But he didn't want them all to have died for nothing, and he didn't want the loose end of Allison lurking around, being all unpredictable. So he was willing to risk losing a few more.

He was at the campground. He'd managed to gather about

thirty men. Many of them were not his employees, but he'd called in a couple of favors and acquired more reinforcements. A couple of them would actively guard Cody and Maggie in their cabin, which was one of sixteen units. Unless she could see through walls, Allison would have a difficult time locating them.

He'd considered leaving Maggie here. Allison had no bond with her, and in fact might wish her nothing but the worst. Still, Maggie was pregnant, and was Allison so far gone that she would let something awful happen to a pregnant woman, even one who was a despicable human being?

Maybe. Maybe not. It gave Winlaw one extra possible advantage.

He'd taken away all of the guns, which did not make the men very happy. If this went anything like the raid on her home, he didn't want anybody panicking and deciding that she was too dangerous to live. *He* would be the one to decide that. If things got too out of control, Matt and Vincent were authorized to shoot her in the head. They were good shots.

He could only get a couple of tranquilizer dart rifles on such short notice. He was, however, able to get a bottle of ketamine and enough hypodermic needles to go around. With so many people attacking her at once, surely at least one of them could inject her.

It was definitely not ideal. With more time, he could probably come up with an infinitely better way to incapacitate and capture her—figure out a way to block her powers, if she actually had them—but on such short notice, he had to go with "She can't possibly kill thirty men at once."

"This is fucked up," said one of the men guarding Cody and Maggie.

"He didn't say to kill them," said his partner. "Just to watch them."

"It's still fucked up. I don't care if I have to shoot *him*," the first man said, pointing his gun at Cody, "but I didn't get into this business to shoot a pregnant lady."

"Again, he didn't say to kill them."

"If she makes a run for it, we'll have to kill her."

The second man nodded. "That's true."

"And I didn't get into this business to do that."

"You didn't get into this business on purpose, did you? You didn't go to college to get a bachelor's degree in drug distribution."

"Shut up. Why are you talking about this in front of them?"

"What difference does that make?"

"You want them to know our business?"

"They're hostages. We're talking about maybe having to kill them. You think it's the drug angle that will make us seem like unsavory guys?"

"I think you should just shut the fuck up."

"Fine. I'll shut the fuck up. We can sit here in silence."

"I'm cool with that."

The men sat there in silence.

Cody and Maggie sat in silence as well. Their hands and feet were still duct-taped together, and they were on the floor, leaning against the cabin wall. It was a one-room cabin that needed some serious dusting, and he'd counted four spiders since they were led in here at gunpoint.

The thought that Allison would save them seemed pretty

ridiculous. He'd come up with an idea, and Maggie had said she was receptive to giving it a try when the time was right, but it was a token gesture, and the odds were that they wouldn't survive until nightfall.

ALLISON PARKED behind the two-story building. The front of the building said Two Nephews Inc., a name that would not fill people with an intense desire to know what kind of business went on within the walls.

"I'm here," she told Winlaw on the phone.

"Are you still in your car?"

"Yes."

"Get out."

Allison got out of the car. "Okay."

"Walk up to the door."

Allison walked up to the door. There was a security camera mounted above it. "I'm there."

WINLAW KNEW SHE WAS. He could see her.

"Knock on the door," he told her.

"What's inside?"

"Two of my associates. They'll take you to where Cody is being held."

"How about we skip this step and you tell me where he is?"

"How about you stay on the phone for a minute, and then you can listen to me slice off Cody's lower lip? Then we'll do a video chat and you can watch me slice off his upper lip. That'll leave his teeth nice and exposed. You like removing people's teeth, don't you?"

"I just like kicking them in the mouth. Whether the teeth stay in place is irrelevant."

"I was going to use a chisel and a claw hammer."

"How about you text me a picture of that chisel and claw hammer right now?"

Winlaw grinned. He wasn't bluffing. He was absolutely prepared to knock out Cody's teeth if necessary. The chisel and hammer, among other tools, were on the table next to him. He took a quick picture and sent it to her.

"What do you think?"

"Send another picture, where the chisel is on top of the hammer like an X."

Winlaw did that. "I don't think it would've been possible to do an image search that quickly, but kudos to you anyway for trying to keep me honest."

OKAY. He was serious.

She'd have to play along for now. She knocked on the door.

It opened right away. A man who looked like an action movie star whose name she couldn't remember stood there.

Stay calm. You're in no danger right now. Don't hurt him.

"I'm here to—" she started to say.

"I know why you're here." He stepped out of her way and gestured for her to enter.

Allison walked into the garage. There was room for about six cars, though none of them were currently parked inside. There wasn't much of anything, really, besides a second man, wearing a black leather jacket, pointing a gun at her. Oh, and a camera in each corner, enclosed in a sphere like the security cameras in department stores.

She wondered why there was this extra stop. Maybe the location where Cody was being held was top-secret, and she'd be blindfolded so that she couldn't find her way back with the authorities. Or maybe he wanted her to face off against two of his men on-camera, so he could actually see what she could do.

The top-secret location idea seemed more likely, but she'd wait to see how this played out.

"Put the gun down," she told the second man. "It makes me nervous."

"It's supposed to make you nervous."

"The other men your boss sent after me made me nervous. It didn't work out very well for them."

The man did not lower his gun. "Get down on your knees."

"You first."

"Do you want to get shot?"

"No," said Allison. "I do not want to get shot. I also don't want you to get in trouble for shooting me. I'm not sure I could live with the guilt if you got scolded on my behalf."

"I'm going to tell you one more time to get down on your knees," the man said.

"What happens when I'm down there?"

"We're going to frisk you, then bind your hands behind your back."

"Yeah, see, that doesn't really work for me. What else could we do instead?"

"Are you insane?" the man asked.

"I can neither confirm nor deny that."

"You're starting to piss me off."

"What if I said I wasn't insane, but then I displayed behavior that made it clear that I was batshit bugfuck crazy? I'd have betrayed your trust."

The man kept the gun pointed at her, but he was obviously trying to figure out how to remain menacing while following his instructions not to actually shoot her.

But then he put the gun in his inside jacket pocket and took out a knife instead. He removed it from its leather sheath, revealing an eight-inch silver blade. "All right," he said. "You caught me. I'd never shoot a woman. I'll give you a fair chance."

He walked toward her.

Allison dropped to her knees. "You win."

If he was allowed to stab her but not shoot her, maybe the other option was correct, that Winlaw was watching to see how she handled this situation. His plan would be much different if she demonstrated supernatural abilities than if she was merely very talented at killing people. She'd have to make him believe the latter.

She couldn't let them bind her hands behind her back.

She adjusted her position a bit. There was a camera in every corner, but they wouldn't provide a perfect view of everything that was happening. Though she couldn't hide anything completely, she could give Winlaw a somewhat obscured angle of her back.

This was still going to be tricky. She'd find out just how well all of her practice on Buster had worked.

The man who looked like an action movie star walked up behind her.

She reached back and grabbed his arm.

Under normal circumstances, grabbing the arm of a guy like that would do absolutely nothing. One second later she'd be facedown on the cement floor with his knee pressed into her back. She needed to both use her ability and demonstrate a fair amount of dexterity, all while being conscious of the camera angle.

Allison stood up as she broke his arm.

She didn't let go, moving as if she'd broken the limb with her hands instead of her mind. One smooth motion. With the speed and the angle, Winlaw shouldn't be able to tell exactly what had happened. And maybe he'd wonder why she held his arm if she could just snap it through telekinesis?

The man howled in pain. He stumbled away from her, his arm dangling uselessly, a large piece of bone protruding from his elbow.

Too bad he didn't get a chance to frisk her.

She reached underneath her shirt and quickly pulled out Buster's gun. She shot at the other man first, just in case he decided to use his own weapon. Not the shot she wanted—she got him in the shoulder. She fired again and shot him in the chin. He pulled the trigger, but his gun was pointed at the floor. As his body fell, she shoved the barrel of the gun against the broken-armed man's chest and fired. She fired twice more as he stood there, mouth wide open. He dropped to his knees and she finished him off with a shot to the head.

Then she took out her phone and called Winlaw.

WINLAW STARED at the live video feed on his computer screen.

What the hell had just happened?

He'd been prepared for Glenn and Rory to die, but he hadn't expected it to go down like this. His fatal flaw had been assuming that having a gun pointed at her would either make her behave or make her use her powers.

As far as he could tell, she was very strong, had very fast reflexes, and knew how to pull a trigger. Was it simply that his men were incompetent?

He answered her call.

"Hi," she said.

"Hi."

"So, it's like this. I knocked on the door, and these guys let me in, and they wanted to tie my hands behind my back—or bind them, or whatever. They weren't specific. That didn't really work for me. One of them kind of left his arm unprotected, and those things break pretty easily if you twist them behind somebody's back. God didn't really intend for them to bend that way. Long story short, they didn't get a chance to frisk me for weapons, which was unfortunate for them because I had a weapon. A few shots later, yadda yadda yadda, they're dead."

"I see."

"I don't get why you keep underestimating me. Is it because I'm a girl? Or do you think maybe all of the people I've killed recently are so entranced by my goddess-like beauty that they don't fight back? I'm no feminist—I'll totally take that as a compliment."

"Are you finished?" Winlaw asked.

"No," said Allison. "I'm actually very angry right now, and I'm tired of your bullshit. No more games. Tell me where you're keeping Cody. If you try any other tricks, I'm gone. Back on the road. You'll never see me again. But you will see a lot of FBI agents at your front door."

"And then Cody will—"

"He'll die. I know. I get it. But I'm not going to let you keep jerking me around. This is it, Winlaw. Your final chance. Tell me where the fuck you are."

"Do you know where the Angela Wood Campground is?"

"No. I can pull it up on the phone's GPS, though."

"You're not far. Twenty minutes. Go straight there. Make any detours or stops, and I'll cut my losses and that will be the end of Cody."

"I accept your terms."

"CAN'T you move me to a chair?" Maggie asked.

"Nope," said one of the men guarding them.

"I can't keep sitting on the floor. It's killing me."

This wasn't part of their plan. Cody could tell that she really was in agony. Her forehead glistened with perspiration.

"Not my problem."

"What kind of animal are you?"

The guard grinned. "Animal. I like that."

His walkie-talkie crackled. A voice sounded over it: "Heads up, everybody. She's here."

25

The campground was easy to find. Allison parked in a lot that was filled with other cars, though she wasn't sure if they belonged to innocent campers or bad guys. She had the eight-inch knife, but it probably wasn't a good idea to go around slashing tires. She didn't want the negotiation to start off on an unpleasant note, and if the criminals wanted to flee from her wrath, she should let them.

She reached over and scratched the top of Spiral's head. She wasn't sure what to do about the cat. If she never returned, she didn't want him to be trapped in the car, to be discovered by Winlaw or one of his men. But if she set him free, he was pretty much screwed. If there'd been time for a side trip, she would've dropped him off at an animal shelter with a promise to claim him after the bloodbath, but she didn't have any real choice but to leave him in the car and hope for the best.

She put out food, water, and kitty litter, then walked away from the car.

Up ahead, a dirt path ran through the center of this area of the campground, with small cabins on each side.

The phone rang. Winlaw, of course. "Am I in the right place?" she asked.

"Yes."

"What now?"

"I'd like you to surrender."

"Bring Cody out and I'll consider it."

"How do I know you won't start killing people left and right?"

"That doesn't sound like me," said Allison. "Oh, wait, yes it does. I'm done playing around. Bring him out, right now, or I'm going to disturb the peace."

"Or, you could surrender, right now. Otherwise we'll roll his severed head at you like a bowling ball."

"It won't go very far on the dirt."

"I feel like you aren't taking me seriously."

"I feel like you expect me to just hand total victory over to you. You wanted to have a face-to-face conversation, and I'm here. Let's do it. I came here to talk. I didn't come here to surrender."

"I'm not sure it's safe for me to talk to you face-to-face," said Winlaw.

"You'll be fine. Just keep your arm out of reach."

"How about I throw you a bone?"

"To break?"

Winlaw chuckled. "Good one."

"Not really. Don't patronize me."

"I'll prove to you that Cody is alive and well. Then we'll talk. Is that acceptable to you?"

"Sure."

Winlaw didn't want Allison to know which cabin Cody was being held in, but he'd known that he might have to give her this information to keep the conversation going. He switched to the walkie-talkie. "Take Cody outside. Keep him out there just long enough for them to make eye contact, then bring him back inside."

Allison saw the door open to the cabin furthest away from her. Cody walked—no, *hopped*—outside, accompanied by one of Winlaw's scumbags. He had duct tape binding his hands and feet. He was too far away for Allison to see his facial expression, though "scared" was probably a good guess. He looked reasonably unharmed.

The scumbag took Cody back inside and closed the door.

"Satisfied?" Winlaw asked over the phone.

"For now. Where do you want to talk?"

"The first cabin on your right."

"Prove to me that you're in there."

"And how would you like me to do that?"

"Are you fucking kidding me?" Allison asked. "You open the door and wave, asshole. How stupid do you think I am? You think I'm just going to wander into a trap?"

"Maybe you already have."

"And maybe I'll leave Cody behind and go right back to my car."

"I'm sure that wouldn't impact your ability to sleep at night. I apologize, this whole thing is becoming antagonistic. It's not going at all the way I'd intended. What I'd like to do, Allison, is offer you a generous salary and all the security you could ever want."

"What, you mean, like, secret service? A 401K?"

"You'll be safe."

"From who?"

"From the world."

"So let me get this straight. You want me to work for you because I've demonstrated a charming ability to kill people, and you obviously have people you'd like to see killed. Maybe you'd like to see the competition wiped out, so you're looking for an assassin-for-hire. I'm a good choice because I look like a helpless middle-aged lady, but the military trained me very well in the art of breaking bones."

"Which branch?" asked Winlaw.

"None of your business. The bone-breaking branch."

"I'd make it worth your while."

"What kind of people would I have to kill?"

"The kind who deserve it."

"So, pedophiles and rapists? Not your competition? Or are pedophiles and rapists your client base?"

"I don't have a kill list. I'd use you when necessary. Otherwise, you could do whatever you want. A life of leisure and luxury. Stick with Cody if you want, or trade up. Anything you want."

"That does sound delightful," said Allison. "You get me Chris

Evans and we've got a deal. No, Chris Hemsworth. No, Chris Pratt. No, all three. You get me all three of them and we've *so* got a deal."

"Are you ready to take this seriously?"

"Almost."

"This offer won't last very long."

"Here's my counter-offer. Let Cody go, and I'll think about it. This offer also won't last very long. In fact, I'll give you thirty seconds to decide."

"And if I say no?"

"I leave."

"Abandoning Cody?"

"I already said I'd do that. Like, more than once. It's not new information at this point. I'd hate to think you weren't paying attention to me."

"Are my thirty seconds up?"

"Getting close."

"Can I have another thirty?"

"Nope."

"That's harsh of you," said Winlaw.

"When are we going to stop all of this flirting and just admit that we're in love with each other?"

Winlaw chuckled. "Amusing."

"Your time is up. Let Cody go."

"Or else you'll leave?"

"Right. Or maybe I'll be really unhappy. You don't want to find out how much of a bitch I can be."

Winlaw didn't respond.

"You still there?" Allison asked.

"Sorry, I had to put you on mute for a moment."

A man stepped into view from behind one of the cabins. Then another. Then another. Within the next few seconds, about twenty-five people had stepped into the path between the cabins.

Okay. This was going to be a bit of a challenge.

"I'm going to give you another chance to surrender," said Winlaw.

"I have to hang up now," Allison informed him. She disconnected the call and shoved the phone into her back pocket.

All right. She'd expected Cody to be guarded by fewer people. There were *way* more guys here than she'd taken out in her home, and there she'd had the benefit of the kitchen doorway, forcing them to go after her one at a time.

But she wasn't going to surrender.

And she wasn't going to run.

In a best-case scenario, she'd really fuck up the closest guy, and everybody else would say, "*Whoa! Let's get out of here, fellas!*" and beat a hasty retreat.

It could happen.

Most likely not.

Allison took a deep breath. She really did not want to die today. But, screw it, it was time to find out just how powerful she truly was.

She walked forward.

The group of men walked toward her.

She didn't see any guns. That was a promising sign that they were still in kidnap mode instead of kill mode. A lot of them did seem to be holding...were those hypodermic needles?

Allison had a very definite phobia of needles. It kept her from seeing a doctor, because the needles would create intense anxiety, and the anxiety would kill doctors. She'd known that she'd eventually have to get over it, but she'd expected that moment to happen in a doctor's office where a kindly physician assured her that it would just be a tiny pinch, not at a campground with twenty-five needle-wielding psychos coming toward her.

She took another deep breath.

"Hey!" she shouted at the group, which was only about fifty feet away. They'd laugh at what she was about to say, but she'd feel better if she gave them a fair warning. "If you have families, this is your chance to leave. If you have spouses or kids or anybody who depends on you, I'm asking you to think about them before this goes any further. I don't want to create widows or orphans. If you don't have good medical coverage or a life insurance plan, that's also something to consider. If this goes further, you're making your own conscious decision for it to happen, and you all need to weigh your personal responsibility to your loved ones when you make your choice. I'm not trying to devalue your lives if you're single—I'm single, I've been that way forever, and trust me, I get it. I know I'm being kind of long-winded here, so what I'm basically saying is that if you come any closer I'm going to kill all of you, and I now consider you all duly warned of the risk."

They didn't all burst into hysterical laughter, though Allison saw a lot of smiles.

Nobody left the group.

Very well, then.

She ran toward them.

MAGGIE WINCED. "AH, CRAP," she said. "*Crap.*"

"What's wrong with you?" one of the men guarding them asked.

She ignored the question and let out a groan of pain.

"You okay?" Cody asked, even though he knew she was.

"I think the baby is coming!"

"Are you serious? Now?"

Maggie frantically nodded.

"The baby is coming!" Cody told the guards, not that they needed the reminder, because they both looked rather horrified. "Go get somebody!"

"Who are we supposed to get?"

"Anybody who knows what they're doing! Hurry up! She's having the baby early because of all the stress you put her through!"

The men looked at each other. Then one of them picked up the walkie-talkie.

"Uh, Mr. Winlaw?"

"What?"

"We've got a problem here with the hostages. A possible live birth situation."

"Excuse me?"

"The pregnant lady seems to be going into labor."

"Handle it."

"Understood, sir. But, uh, more information on how we should handle it would be appreciated."

"*Handle it.* I don't have time for this."

The man set the walkie-talkie back down, looking panicked.

Maggie squeezed her eyes shut and cried out in pain.

It looked like she'd wet her pants. Cody hadn't expected her to pee herself to make it look like her water had broken, but he appreciated the extra effort.

She opened her eyes and looked over at him. "*It's really happening.*"

Oh, shit.

That wasn't good.

"We need to get her to a hospital!" Cody said.

The man who'd spoken with Winlaw shook his head. Even in the bad light, Cody could see that he'd gone completely pale. "She's not going anywhere."

"She's having a baby!"

"I know that! Her timing sucks! There's nothing we can do!"

Maggie cried out again.

Then, outside the cabin, Cody heard even more screams.

26

Allison let out a shriek and waved both of her hands in the air, as if she was trying to part the Red Sea.

The crowd of men did not part, but three or four of them in the front let out shrieks of their own as their arms twisted around. Though she couldn't hear the cracking sounds over all of the other noise, she was confident that they were quite loud.

She stopped running.

She waved her hands again, trying to imagine a wave of energy flowing through them to the legs of her closest attackers. One of the men's legs bent upwards, like he was trying to kick himself in the face. He bellowed in pain and fell forward, landing hard on that very leg, sending a spurt of blood flying from his knee.

The men on either side of him suffered very similar fates. One hit the ground with such a strong impact that if they'd been on concrete instead of dirt, she believed that his face would have burst open like a water balloon. Even on this softer surface, plenty of blood was gushing from his nose as he lifted his head to scream.

And now some of the men behind them tripped over their fallen comrades. Others stopped, because they hadn't expected the men in front to start screaming before they even reached their target.

Allison shrieked again, the better to harness all of the chaos she felt inside, and slashed at the air. She was a vicious lioness, clawing at her prey.

Bones were breaking all over the place. Fingers, wrists, arms, shoulders.

She kept slashing. Ribs, hips, legs, feet.

Men kept dropping to the ground, clutching their broken limbs.

She'd warned them. Nobody could say she hadn't warned them.

She kept shrieking, even though her throat was already beginning to hurt, and waved even more frantically. One man's jaw snapped down, splitting his cheeks. Another had a bone burst through the side of his neck. Another had both of his legs snap at once, down at the shins, like he was doing some sort of crazy dance move.

Allison took a few steps back.

How many men were on the ground already? Ten? Eleven? Not quite half, but she'd made a serious dent in their ranks. And the ones who remained upright seemed to be very unsure of themselves.

A dart flew past her, almost hitting her in the neck.

Oh, hell no.

Who was holding it? It was a guy off to the side, not far away, and he probably would have hit her for sure if he'd been able to more calmly take aim. Presumably it was a tranquilizer dart. She couldn't have that.

She swung her fist at him, as if trying to punch him from a distance.

His forehead burst open. It was as if she'd bashed him with an iron mallet as hard as she possibly could. He fell onto his back and did not make another attempt to fire at her with the tranquilizer gun.

Was he the only one who had one of those?

Unlikely.

She scanned the bloody crowd. Yep, there was another guy pointing one at her. She swiped her hand, and his aim changed, causing him to shoot the guy in front of him. That wasn't Allison's intention, but it worked well enough, she supposed. He still had the gun, though. She squeezed her fist, and his entire arm turned red. He dropped the gun.

Allison continued waving her arms, conducting her symphony of carnage.

Winlaw sat by the window of his cabin, watching the encounter outside.

This was going, very, very badly.

She was more powerful than he could ever have imagined, and he no longer wanted anything to do with her. He'd assumed that he could control her. He couldn't control somebody who was out there slaughtering two-dozen men without even touching them.

He wasn't sure if he should order them to retreat, and try to salvage a small portion of his workforce, or just tell them to kill her.

Better to have them kill her.

"WHAT THE HELL is going on out there?" asked one of the guards.

"Who gives a shit?" asked his partner, pointing to Maggie. "I didn't sign up for this! We can't just stand here and watch while she has a baby on the floor!"

"No, you can't!" said Cody. "Cut her feet free!"

"We can't do that."

"You think she's going to run away while she's giving birth? Cut her goddamn feet free! What's the matter with you?"

The guard stood there for a moment, frozen in indecision. Then he cut the duct tape binding Maggie's feet.

If Maggie had been faking her labor pains, as originally planned, this would be the moment where she took surprise action against their captors. Instead, she spread her legs and continued to cry out in pain.

ALLISON FLUNG one of the men into the air. He didn't get a lot of height, seven or eight feet, but he crashed down upon two of the other men who'd still been standing.

With even more practice, Allison might one day be able to lift an entire group of twenty-five men high into the air. Release them and let them all splatter to the ground. Problem solved.

One man got close enough to grab her arm.

She grabbed the arm that had grabbed her arm.

Then she tugged on it.

Her mind did most of the work, but his entire arm tore off at the shoulder. She tossed it away instead of beating him with it.

She wondered if she could do that again with his other arm.

Yep, she could.

The armless man wasn't dead yet, but he would be soon enough, so she had to turn her attention to other problems. Another man jabbed at her with his needle, and she flinched with fear at the near-miss. His eyeballs burst. Not what she'd meant to make happen.

A couple of men near the back turned and ran. Allison didn't blame them. And if they'd run away as soon as the grisly events in the Angela Wood Campground began, she might have let them go. But in her own self-interest, and that of Cody, she had to make sure they weren't running off to get a machine gun or something, and therefore they needed to die.

Could she break their backs from this distance?

She made a gesture that approximated what she'd do if they were right in front of her and she was trying to snap their spinal columns with her bare hands. It didn't work. A guy closer to her did suddenly lurch forward with a huge red splotch on the front of his shirt, like the moment right before the chest-burster made its appearance in *Alien*.

She tried again.

Their backs didn't break, at least not as far as she could tell, but one's legs broke and the other's neck snapped. It was weird that she made the same gesture with both hands and yet one impacted a man's legs and the other impacted a man's neck, but she was still new to wholesale slaughter.

Most of the men were lying on the ground. Not many of them were dead—they were mostly just broken and mangled and not much of a problem for her at the moment.

She stepped over one, and he immediately slammed a hypodermic needle into her leg.

It didn't sting, though. As far as she could tell, the needle broke off on her jeans instead of puncturing her calf. She punched down. He gasped for breath as his hands went to his broken windpipe.

One guy, not learning the lesson of everybody around him, let out some sort of battle cry and rushed at her, a hypodermic needle held mightily above his head. She broke his arm, then flung him into the air, where he landed upon the most mangled of the corpses.

Only six or seven men were left.

After breaking a neck, they were easier to count. Six left.

"Take her panties off!" Cody said.

The guard hesitated.

"She can't have a baby through her underwear! Jesus Christ! Cut me free! I'll take care of it!"

"Not a chance," the guard informed him.

"Then handle it! Get some warm water! Get a towel!"

"We weren't prepared for this!"

"Then maybe you shouldn't have brought a pregnant woman out to a cabin! This is on you!"

"I'm not hearing as many screams outside," said the other guard. "I don't like it."

"Don't worry about what's happening outside," Cody told him. "Worry about what's happening right here in front of you. You assholes get to be honorary obstetricians, so you'd better rise to the occasion!"

The first guard reached under Maggie's dressed and pulled off her panties.

"It's coming!" Maggie wailed, clenching her fists so tightly that Cody was confident she would have smashed his bones into powder if he were holding her hand and telling her to breathe.

The guard looked. "Oh, shit, it really is!"

WINLAW WAS REPEATEDLY GIVING the order to kill, yet nobody was paying attention to the walkie-talkies. He could open the door and shout it out, but as of the last couple of minutes he was not very keen on giving away his location. He should have stayed back at his office. How could he have possibly known that twenty-five men wouldn't be enough?

He did have a very solid answer about whether it was telekinesis or military training, not that it mattered anymore.

He'd just have to wait here and hope that her rampage did not involve going cabin to cabin seeking new victims.

Only four men remained upright, and one of them was limping pretty bad, while another had a dangling arm with no fewer than three visible bones protruding through his shirt. None of them were currently trying to attack her.

"*Please*," one of them said. "*Enough*."

Allison broke his neck.

"You're a fucking monster," another said.

"I gave you a warning. I stood right over there and gave a great big speech offering you the chance to bail. I mean, yeah, I would've been dubious, too, but it was twenty-five of you against one woman. If your boss was that scared of me, shouldn't you have realized that this wasn't a great place to be?"

"I surrender," said the one who'd said *please* and *enough*.

"I don't accept your surrender," Allison told him. "I don't want any prisoners, and I don't want anybody around to vow vengeance against me."

She broke his shoulder, then recalibrated and broke his neck.

"You'll rot in hell for this," the man who'd called her a monster said.

She broke his neck as well.

She didn't like being a cold-blooded killer. She'd been left with no choice. If Winlaw had brought a hundred men here, she would have killed all hundred of them. If he'd brought two, there'd only be two fatalities. This was on him.

She slammed the two remaining men into each other as hard as she could. They didn't fall, so she did it a few more times, until they dropped to the ground.

Allison knew that she was going to have a very hard time coping with what she'd done once she was removed from the immediacy of the situation. Warning or not, she'd murdered a hell of a lot of people in a brutal manner, and she'd be having nightmares about this for the rest of her life. The whole cliché of seeing it every time she closed her eyes might be entirely accurate. This was going to haunt her.

Especially the next part.

Because she couldn't have the men who were still alive going to the hospital and speaking about what had happened. Describing her. Taking away her ability to run away from this forever.

She cracked her knuckles, and violently waved her hands back and forth.

Bones shattered. Blood sprayed into the air as the men came apart. Limbs separated from bodies. Heads were torn off by her invisible hands.

The moans of agony grew quieter.

Soon the men were silent enough that she could hear the bones breaking. Maybe even hear the flow of blood, though that may have been her imagination.

She kept going, covering the entire area in front of her, until the bodies weren't simply dead, they were unrecognizable. It was going to take a lot of time and effort to sort out the individual people who were in this pile of gore.

Finally, it was time to quit. All she could hear was a ringing in her ears.

No. There were more cries of pain. A woman. Coming from one of the cabins near the back.

She ran toward it.

The door to a different cabin opened. A man stepped out.

Though she'd made up her own mental picture, it occurred

to her that she didn't actually know what Winlaw looked like. She was almost positive this was him, though.

She tried to break his neck.

He was too far away.

He pointed a gun at her.

Allison desperately tried to break his arm before he could squeeze the trigger.

He fired.

Allison fell.

27

"Cut my hands free, for God's sake!" Cody shouted. "If you're not going to help, let me do it! I've delivered babies before! You want the death of a preemie on your conscience?"

The first guard, who'd slammed his hand over his mouth and gagged a few times but hadn't actually thrown up, shook his head.

"You're going to let the baby be born on a filthy floor? Let me *help!*"

"Let him help," said the second guard, who looked queasy.

"I'll cut your hands loose but not your feet," said the first guard. "Try anything and this knife goes into your face."

Cody decided not to try anything.

ALLISON SAT UP.

She couldn't feel anything, but he'd hit her right beneath the collarbone and it was bad.

Winlaw hadn't lowered the gun.

Allison had never been so frightened or angry in her life. After all of this, it ended with her getting shot, and the certain execution of Cody. And now the pain was starting—it had just taken a moment to kick in.

Pain. Fear. Anger.

She stared right at Winlaw and swiped at him.

His entire face tore off.

He dropped the gun.

She swiped again.

Because he was wearing a shirt, she couldn't see exactly what happened to his chest, but the shirt immediately turned red and parts began to spew out from the bottom. She could only identify his intestines for certain.

WINLAW DROPPED TO HIS KNEES. He tried to cross his arms over his stomach to keep everything inside, but that wasn't working at all, and his face was within reach and maybe he should try to pick it up, no, that was stupid, but it was getting all dirty, could you graft somebody's face back on, was he going to die, yes, he was going to die, he hoped Olivia got her revenge on Daxton, he hoped she made him suffer, oh God his face hurt, he wasn't going to be able to keep his balance much longer, maybe it was time to just give up and die, yeah, death sounded good, good-bye...

THE CABIN DOOR OPENED.

Thick wounds appeared across both guards' necks, like a ghost had slashed their throats.

Allison stepped into the cabin. She'd been shot and looked like a scary crazy woman, but Cody had never been more relieved to see anybody in his life.

Allison looked at Maggie. "Is she—?"

"Yeah."

"Can you handle it?"

"Yeah."

"All right. I'm going to get some duct tape for my bullet hole. I'll be back."

MAGGIE LEANED AGAINST THE WALL, holding her baby. Cody had decided not to cut the umbilical cord with a germ-laden knife, so it was a pretty nasty sight, but as far as he could tell, the baby was healthy.

"I'm going to find Allison," Cody told her. "She's been gone too long."

"No, I'm here," said Allison, stepping into the cabin. Her wound had indeed been duct-taped up. "Just a little slow and woozy."

Maggie's eyes went wide with fright. "Please, please, please don't hurt me," she begged.

Allison crouched down next to her. "You don't deserve to live."

Maggie held up her newborn. "But she's innocent."

"And that is why I'm going to have mercy on you. You get to live. And you are going to do what it takes to be the best fucking mother on the planet. Mother of the Year. I'll check up on you. Consider me your homicidal child protection services. Because this kid is the *only* reason you're not on the pile of corpses with the rest of them, and I reserve the right to change my mind any fucking time I want. Whatever Winlaw was going to do to you, I'll do much worse. Are we totally clear on this?"

Maggie vigorously nodded.

Allison turned to Cody. "It's a bad mess out there. However gruesome you think it is, double that image in your mind. Triple it. Really all I need from you is to keep your mouth shut. You were never here. You were never kidnapped. Whatever conclusion is drawn when people analyze the splatter out there, they won't guess correctly. Everybody who could tie me to this is dead. I didn't even use my own phone to talk to them. Maybe I can salvage my old life, even keep my job as long as I don't get laid off, but I'm going to disappear for a while."

"I'll go with you."

"No."

"But—"

"It can't work between us. I'm going to have to reconcile the fact that I killed a lot—a *lot*—of people on purpose, but I refuse to risk killing you by accident. I shouldn't even be talking to you right now. I have to go."

"But you've been shot."

Allison glanced down at the taped-up bullet wound. "Yeah, I'm gonna have to find one of those doctors who don't ask questions. Wish I'd gotten a referral before I killed everybody around here. I'll figure it out. I've got the Internet."

"All right," said Cody. "Be careful."

"I always am. I mean, not so much today, but overall, in general, I'm careful."

"You don't have to tell me where you are, but will you let me know that you're okay?"

"I'll try." Allison stood up and walked toward the doorway. Then she stopped and turned back around. She looked down at Maggie. "I'm going to need a favor from you."

Daxton looked at his cell phone. A text from Maggie. There was a picture attached.

He almost dropped the phone when he saw it. She was holding a baby.

He immediately called her.

"Oh my God," she said. "It's been...I can't even describe how it's been. Mr. Winlaw! He went insane! He kidnapped me! I barely got away!"

Wait, did she not know he knew she'd been abducted? Did Winlaw not tell her?

"What the hell are you talking about?" he asked.

"He kidnapped me and locked me in a room, but the baby came early, and he had to help deliver it, and then I just ran! He's going to come after us! Daxton, you have to come pick me up as soon as you can! We have to run! We have to get our baby away from him!"

Was this possible? Was he going to have a happy ending after all? All he'd wanted in the first place was to take Maggie and get the hell out of town. He'd go get her and his daughter, then drive somewhere that Mr. Winlaw would never, ever find them.

"Where are you?"

EPILOGUE

THREE MONTHS LATER

Allison lay on the couch, legs wide open as she imagined Cody on top of her, kissing her neck as he thrust into her.

The vibrator hummed. It was a top of the line model and worth every penny. She'd bought a couple of other expensive ones that didn't quite do the trick, but this one was absolutely stellar. She would leave a five-star online review later tonight.

She whimpered. She was getting so close.

So close.

Almost there.

Her legs began to tremble.

When the orgasm hit, she completely let herself go, thrashing around on the couch as she cried out in pleasure.

It took her a few moments to calm down. She just lay there, panting.

She turned off the vibrator, set it aside, and got up off the couch in the basement. She pulled her dress down and smoothed it out. Then she walked around to the other side of the curtain.

"Anything?" she asked.

Daxton didn't answer. Of course, he couldn't speak, not with his mouth taped shut, but she'd learned from previous experiments that she couldn't climax if he was making disparaging comments, so she had to muffle him.

He was chained to a steel table. He wore only a pair of boxer shorts—not because of anything kinky, but so she could more easily check him for injuries. His broken legs weren't healing very well. Allison was no medical professional and she didn't know how to set a broken bone, especially one that had burst through the skin. His arms were also looking pretty bad.

He'd stopped coughing up blood a few days ago, so that was good.

Of course, right now she didn't care about the older injuries. She cared about new ones. She didn't see any that hadn't been there before she used the vibrator.

"I asked you a question," she said. "Did you feel anything break?"

Daxton shook his head.

He wouldn't lie to her. Not again.

"That's great news," she said. It was amazing how quickly she was improving her skills when she could practice on a daily basis. Oh, there was still plenty of work to do, but this was the third time she'd had an orgasm with only the privacy curtain separating her and Daxton without him suffering any new injuries.

She was really learning to control this.

She was on her way to a much happier life.

"I'm making a lot of progress, thanks to you," she told Daxton. "I can't wait to give Cody the latest update." She looked over at the clock. "He's not quite off work yet, so I guess I'll try it one more time. Practice makes perfect."

— The End —

ACKNOWLEDGMENTS

Thanks to Tod Clark, Donna Fitzpatrick, Paul Goblirsch, Lynne Hansen, Michael McBride, Jim Morey, Rhonda Rettig, and Paul Synuria II for their bone-breaking assistance with this novel.

BOOKS BY JEFF STRAND

Wolf Hunt 3. George, Lou, Ally, and Eugene are back in another werewolf-laden adventure.

Clowns Vs. Spiders. Choose your side!

My Pretties. A serial kidnapper may have met his match in the two young ladies who walk the city streets at night, using themselves as bait...

Five Novellas. A compilation of *Stalking You Now, An Apocalypse of Our Own, Faint of Heart, Kutter,* and *Facial.*

Ferocious. The creatures of the forest are dead...and hungry!

Bring Her Back. A tale of revenge and madness.

Sick House. A home invasion from beyond the grave.

Bang Up. A filthy comedic thriller. "You want to pay me to sleep with your wife?" is just the start of the story.

Cold Dead Hands. Ten people are trapped in a freezer during a terrorist attack on a grocery store.

How You Ruined My Life (Young Adult). Sixteen-year-old Rod has a pretty cool life until his cousin Blake moves in and slowly destroys everything he holds dear.

Everything Has Teeth. A third collection of short tales of horror and macabre comedy.

An Apocalypse of Our Own. Can the Friend Zone survive the end of the world?

Stranger Things Have Happened (Young Adult). Teenager Marcus

Millian III is determined to be one of the greatest magicians who ever lived. Can he make a live shark disappear from a tank?

Cyclops Road. When newly widowed Evan Portin gives a woman named Harriett a ride out of town, she says she's on a cross-country journey to slay a Cyclops. Is she crazy, or...?

Blister. While on vacation, cartoonist Jason Tray meets the town legend, a hideously disfigured woman who lives in a shed.

The Greatest Zombie Movie Ever (Young Adult). Three best friends with more passion than talent try to make the ultimate zombie epic.

Kumquat. A road trip comedy about TV, hot dogs, death, and obscure fruit.

I Have a Bad Feeling About This (Young Adult). Geeky, non-athletic Henry Lambert is sent to survival camp, which is bad enough *before* the trio of murderous thugs show up.

Pressure. What if your best friend was a killer...and he wanted you to be just like him? Bram Stoker Award nominee for Best Novel.

Dweller. The lifetime story of a boy and his monster. Bram Stoker Award nominee for Best Novel.

A Bad Day For Voodoo. A young adult horror/comedy about why sticking pins in a voodoo doll of your history teacher isn't always the best idea. Bram Stoker Award nominee for Best Young Adult Novel.

Dead Clown Barbecue. A collection of demented stories about severed noses, ventriloquist dummies, giant-sized vampires, sibling stabbings, and lots of other messed-up stuff.

Dead Clown Barbecue Expansion Pack. A few more stories for those who couldn't get enough.

Wolf Hunt. Two thugs for hire. One beautiful woman. And one vicious frickin' werewolf.

Wolf Hunt 2. New wolf. Same George and Lou.

The Sinister Mr. Corpse. The feel-good zombie novel of the year.

Benjamin's Parasite. A rather disgusting action/horror/comedy about why getting infected with a ghastly parasite is unpleasant.

Fangboy. A dark and demented fairy tale for adults.

Facial. Greg has just killed the man he hired to kill one of his wife's many lovers. Greg's brother desperately needs a dead body. It's kind of related to the lion corpse that he found in his basement. This is the normal part of the story.

Kutter. A serial killer finds a Boston terrier, and it might just make him into a better person.

Faint of Heart. To get her kidnapped husband back, Melody has to relive her husband's nightmarish weekend, step-by-step...and survive.

Mandibles. Giant killer ants wreaking havoc in the big city!

Stalking You Now. A twisty-turny thriller soon to be the feature film *Mindy Has To Die.*

Graverobbers Wanted (No Experience Necessary). First in the Andrew Mayhem series.

Single White Psychopath Seeks Same. Second in the Andrew Mayhem series.

Casket For Sale (Only Used Once). Third in the Andrew Mayhem series.

Lost Homicidal Maniac (Answers to "Shirley"). Fourth in the Andrew Mayhem series.

Suckers (with JA Konrath). Andrew Mayhem meets Harry McGlade. Which one will prove to be more incompetent?

Gleefully Macabre Tales. A collection of thirty-two demented tales. Bram Stoker Award nominee for Best Collection.

Elrod McBugle on the Loose. A comedy for kids (and adults who were warped as kids).

The Haunted Forest Tour (with Jim Moore). The greatest theme park attraction in the world! Take a completely safe ride through an actual haunted forest! Just hope that your tram doesn't break down, because this forest is PACKED with monsters...

Draculas (with JA Konrath, Blake Crouch, and F. Paul Wilson). An outbreak of feral vampires in a secluded hospital. This one isn't much like *Twilight.*

Subscribe to Jeff Strand's free monthly newsletter (which includes a brand-new original short story in every issue) at http://eepurl.com/bpv5br

And remember:

Readers who leave reviews deserve great big hugs!

Made in the USA
Middletown, DE
28 April 2020

92323265R00161